T0068133

Part Two

A Young Girl's FANTASY

VANESSA CARNEGIE

ARCHWAY
PUBLISHING

Copyright © 2017 Vanessa Carnegie.

All rights reserved. No part of this book may be used or reproduced by
any means, graphic, electronic, or mechanical, including photocopying,
recording, taping or by any information storage retrieval system
without the written permission of the author except in the case of
brief quotations embodied in critical articles and reviews.

This is a work of fiction. All of the characters, names, incidents,
organizations, and dialogue in this novel are either the products
of the author's imagination or are used fictitiously.

Archway Publishing books may be ordered through booksellers or by contacting:

Archway Publishing
1663 Liberty Drive
Bloomington, IN 47403
www.archwaypublishing.com
1 (888) 242-5904

Because of the dynamic nature of the Internet, any web addresses or
links contained in this book may have changed since publication and
may no longer be valid. The views expressed in this work are solely those
of the author and do not necessarily reflect the views of the publisher,
and the publisher hereby disclaims any responsibility for them.

Any people depicted in stock imagery provided by Thinkstock are models,
and such images are being used for illustrative purposes only.
Certain stock imagery © Thinkstock.

ISBN: 978-1-4808-4329-5 (sc)
ISBN: 978-1-4808-4330-1 (e)

Library of Congress Control Number: 2017903514

Print information available on the last page.

Archway Publishing rev. date: 04/27/2017

A young girl's fantasy can turn into a nightmare!!!!!

ACKNOWLEDGEMENTS

I would like to thank God first. I would like to thank my mom and my sons Ethan and Erick and my fiancé Dorjan and my whole entire family. I love you all! Shout outs to all my friends, and clients and customers. Thanks for all of your support, I love you all!

Christina Brown is young, spoiled and beautiful. She's good at manipulating people and she's good at getting what she wants. When her love life turns sour she decides to move to a new city. Her life takes a turn for the worst when she tries to play the wrong person. Christina is forced to find herself out the drama that she somehow put herself in.

CHAPTER 1

How It All Started

I had a tough life coming up as a child. I was born in raised in San Francisco California There was drama before I even arrived in this world. My dad was killed before I came out of the womb. His supposed best friends Tony and Jason murdered him. They were all hustling together, but my dad had chosen a different lifestyle for himself. He broke away from the streets and started to invest his money. He made it up to be a millionaire. His friends felt like he thought he was better than them; they got jealous and wanted him dead. They stole all the money he left for the family. My mom had a mental breakdown. She became heavily addicted to drugs. She even prostituted to get her fix. There were plenty of nights that she went without feeding me. There were plenty of nights she didn't come home, leaving my older sister Sabrina no choice but to step in. My life was a mess. I was this little kid living in a broken-down apartment with no mother or father and hardly any food or clothing. As a child I was pretty easy going. I didn't complain much. I just sat back and went with the flow.

As soon as my sister was old enough, she got a job and with her small paychecks she bought me food and clothes. When Sabrina became a senior in high school, she and Mom began to fight a lot. Sabrina ran away several times but she always came back because she felt like she was responsible for me. When she turned eighteen, she met a millionaire named Michael during one of her first visits to Los Angeles; Mom had gone out on one of her missions to get high. I remember her being really pissed off because Sabrina was gone and she wanted her to watch me. She got desperate and she left me home alone. I was ten years old at the time. I remember being home alone for two days. I survived by eating cereal and milk and peanut butter and jelly sandwiches, which Sabrina always kept in the house.

Mrs. Jenkins, the older woman who lived next door came to check on things as she would normally and she found me home alone. When she found me, she was angry. She called the police and reported my mom as a missing person. Next thing I knew I was getting picked up by Child protective Services and placed in a group home. I was in a group home for a year. That's when things started to change for me. Even though I was raised in the ghetto and I grew up with my mom being on drugs, I was still somehow sheltered from the street life. I hated people on drugs and I stayed away from trouble. My sister made sure I grew up feeling somewhat normal and Mrs. Jenkins made sure we were in church every single Sunday.

The group home that I lived in was clean and well-ordered. The staff really tried their best to up keep the place. They wanted us to feel as comfortable as possible. The group home is where I met my two best friends, Carmen and Katrina. We all were the perfect clique; our personalities mixed well. We each had our own separate dramas, which had led us to the home.

Katrina's mom was serving a four- year sentence for theft and possession of crack cocaine. She had no one to take her in. She tried to live with her aunt but was declined. They didn't want anything to do with her because of the things her mom did.

Carmen's situation was a bit different. She was in the group home because she didn't get along with her mom. Her mom was a middle-class woman who worked really hard to make ends meet. She had three other kids and she had no time to put up with the drama that Carmen was trying to throw her way. They'd had so many fights that it was just impossible for the two to live together.

I witnessed a bunch of crazy things during my stay. These girls were absolutely wild and crazy. Their ages ranged between twelve and sixteen. They had all kinds of drugs in and out that place. At night when the staff was asleep, they would sneak their boyfriends inside and they would have sex. Some of the girls had pimps and prostituted on a regular basis.

After a year of living in the group home, things turned around. Mom had gotten clean and Sabrina had retrieved the money that my deceased father had left for us. All of a sudden we were living the good life. We moved into a nice-sized home. I had any and everything that I could have possibly wanted and when I turn eighteen. I have three hundred thousand dollars coming my way.

When Sabrina moved out and had a family of her own it was just me and moms and I was spoiled rotten. She mainly spoiled me because she felt terrible for not being a good mother for all those years. She even gave me the master bedroom, inside it had a balcony, two walk-in closets, a large screen TV, a stereo system, and my very own huge bathroom that had a Jacuzzi that fit up to six people. I knew it was wrong but I took advantage of the situation. I felt that since I didn't have a mother for eleven years I deserved to be a spoiled brat. Even moms knew that. That's why I got any and everything I wanted.

CHAPTER 2

The Present

I was now seventeen and a senior in high school. I had a much different attitude than the one I'd had when I was younger. My sister and I were drifting further apart and moms said I was driving her crazy. I told them they both wouldn't have to worry about me much longer because I was going to be eighteen soon. I was going to be a grown ass woman.

Graduation was coming up and I couldn't wait to be leaving this boring school. School wasn't my thing. I was more of a social bug. I was more into friends and fun, fashion, and of course, boys. In the yearbook I was voted most popular, best dressed, and the prettiest. I was well known and it was a two-way situation with me. It was either you loved me or hated me. There was no in-between and I didn't care one way or another; I was well off. I was the only one in my school driving a brand new shiny red Mercedes Benz. Not even the teacher's rides were as nice as mine. All the guys in the school wanted to date me but I just wasn't interested in any of them. I had my eyes set on older men. I had my own boyfriend, but I still had a huge crush on this guy named Trey. He was twenty-six and he was the owner of the car wash which was two blocks away from where I lived. His businesslike attitude had me checking for him. Now he was what you would call a real man. While the other cats were out trying to sell drugs and be thug, he was handling his business and doing it well. His skin was dark and smooth. He was always dressed fitted from head to toe. He always kept a fresh haircut and his waves were dipping harder than the ocean. He was six-five, tall enough to play in the NBA, and he had a muscular body. I just knew he was packing. Day and night I thought about Trey. I thought of him so much that I completely lost focus in school. I tried to hit on him every time I saw him but he just wasn't feeling me. He said that I was too young and I was much too spoiled and the spoiled part he made very clear. But that didn't stop me from trying. I knew that somehow and some way I was going to get him. In the meantime, I had my own things going on.

Sabrina, my older sister, was starting to work my nerves. She still acted as if she was my mom. She was used to it. She had her hopes on sending me to college. She had money put away in a fund. She made it clear that I wouldn't have any excuses.

Sabrina had it all. She was beautiful and she was highly intelligent. She always made good grades. She had a lot of class and she was well respected in the community. She had a wonderful husband and the perfect child. She was living the typical dream that most women wanted. I loved my sister to death, but at times she could be way too controlling. I didn't want to disappoint her, but I didn't have my heart set on college. College wasn't for everyone, and it certainly wasn't for me. I wanted to be a celebrity. I didn't know exactly what I wanted to do; I just knew I wanted to be famous. I wanted everyone to know who I was. I wanted my picture on the cover of magazines. I daydreamed all the time about walking down the red carpet, photographers wanting to take pictures of me and the best part of it all would be partying with the rappers, singers, ball players, and movie stars.

My dream came to a sudden end when I heard a knock at the door.

"Hey Chrissie, what you been up to?" asked Sabrina.

"Nothing," I said trying not to make eye contact with her.

"Why haven't you been returning my phone calls?" she asked.

I tried to think of an excuse but couldn't come up with anything.

"Let me take a wild guess: you haven't found a school yet?"

"I haven't found anything that I want to dedicate four years of my time to."

"You really don't want to go to college, I can feel it."

She was now getting highly upset.

"Look, I want to break into the Hollywood scene. School is just not going to cut it."

"Okay, so what is it that you want to be?"

"I'm not sure yet."

"You don't even know? Do you have any idea how many people want to become famous? They dedicate all their time in all these acting classes, music lessons, modeling courses, and auditions and they never really become the superstar that they dreamed about being. Look, I respect your dream and all but I just want you to have something to fall back on. At least go to school until you figure out exactly what you want to do."

As mad as she made me sometimes, she did have a solid point about this one.

"I'll start looking."

"Good," she said as she let out a sigh of relief. "I'm going to head on to work now call me later and let me know what school you decide." She then left out the door.

"Damn, she gets on my nerves!" I said to myself as I headed on out to get my car washed and to see Trey.

I pulled up inside the car wash and I got out the car. All the men who came to get their car washed had their eyes glued to me. I even saw one man get slapped by his girlfriend for looking at me so hard.

Everyone had their eyes on me except for the person whom I wanted the attention from. He looked me up and down once and he turned right back on around. I never took these types of things to heart. This was how Trey always treated me. I walked directly toward him.

"What's up Trey?"

"Working hard like always," he said in a serious tone of voice.

"Why do you have to be so stuck up and boring?" I asked him.

"I have fun when the time is right."

"So who's going to wash my car? I didn't like how that guy did it the last time." I was really trying to keep up a conversation. But it was obvious he was trying to make it quick and short like always.

"I will have someone else wash it then, no big deal. In the meantime have a seat in the waiting room and your car will be finished in a little bit."

I was fed up so I blurted out: "Why do you treat me so mean? Am I ugly to you or something?"

"Your attitude is sometimes, but appearance-wise you look alright."

"Just alright? Do you see all that attention I was getting out there? Even if you didn't see it I know you heard all those men trying to hit up on me. Most guys find me very attractive. What in the hell is wrong with you?" I asked.

"I'm not into just looks. I'm looking for more in a woman."

"I have a good heart, I'm nice at times and it's not like I will come into the relationship empty-handed like most of these women. I have a lot to offer a man. I got money and did you check out these curves?"

"Okay, enough. Please have a seat in the waiting room like everyone else."

"Fine," I said as I went inside the waiting room. I looked back to see if he was watching, but of course he was into his work. I wasn't bothered though. It was just one time out of a hundred attempts to get him to notice me. After my car was finished I was supposed to go to school but instead I made a trip to the mall. I bought two new designer bags and I bought a pair of high boots. As I was leaving the shoe store, a guy approached me.

"Hey cutie what's your name?"

When I turned around I wasn't expecting him to be as handsome as he was and normally I wouldn't have even stopped, but the brother caught my attention. He had diamonds on almost everything he owned from his chain to his ring to his watch. He was fitted from head to toe. He was tall and handsome and just my type.

"My name is Cristina."

"Cristina and Chris, I like that," he said with a smile on his face.

"I guess that does sound rather cute," I agreed.

"You're looking sexy as ever and I'm feeling your style. Can I get your number or something?" he asked, as he looked me up and down again.

"How about you give me yours and I will call you later."

"But are you going to call me though? Don't have a brother wasting his time and all." he said as he wrote down his phone number on a small sheet of paper that he found inside his pocket.

"He does look like a keeper." I said to myself as I smiled; I got in my car and drove off.

As soon as I walked in the house my mom was sitting on the couch waiting for me.

"Cristina, we need to have a talk," She said in a serious tone of voice.

"What now, mom?"

"Your school called here today and they said that this was your second day in a row skipping class."

"Shit, I'm busted." I thought to myself.

"Now, I know that I've been pretty lenient on you and you get away with a lot of things, but you're just taking advantage. If I get one more phone call I'm taking that shiny red car of yours."

"No mamma, not the car" I cried.

"Then you need to act like you got some sense!" she said as she left the room.

The next day I got a phone call from the person I did not want to hear from. It was my sister Sabrina.

"What's up with you skipping school? Remember, we talked about you going to college."

"Don't try to act like you ain't ever cut school before, except you used to drink alcohol and smoke weed. I never tried either one." I was lying through my teeth.

"My grades were honor roll grades and you're barely even passing."

"Why do you have to be such a player hater anyway? You're always in my business."

"You better be lucky someone is in your business because I see a disaster coming."

"You're supposed to be my cool older sister. You're supposed to have my back, but instead you act like my mom. Matter of fact, mom's even cooler than you are."

"When you do the right things, I will always have your back and in the meantime, I won't sit there and condone you cutting school."

"Well it just sounds to me that you don't have much of a life."

"You know what little girl I done heard enough from you. You will just have to learn for yourself." She hung up the phone.

Carmen, Katrina and I were the most popular clique in the school. Everyone wanted to be down with us. We were cool fly and every one was trying to bite our style. We always wore the latest. All of our clothes were name brand because we couldn't let down our audience; we had an image we had to maintain.

Every day we would hang out after school. We would either go out to eat or to the mall or we would have a couple of drinks and we would make some dude pay for everything. I had money of my own but it was cool to make the men pay for us.

The men I dated were much older. They had jobs homes and cars unlike these guys that were our age. We were high maintenance chicks; we didn't have time for all that. I wasn't going to let a guy take me out on a date on a bus or in his parent's car or use his lunch money to pay for our date. I was attracted to guys who had good paying incomes. Men who wanted the larger things in life, I was young and all, but I was a little bit ahead of the game. I knew how to invest my money by buying stock, I also knew about mutual funds, and bank CD,s and I also knew a little something about real estate. I knew what it took to start and run a business. I was much smarter than what people gave me credit for. My sister gave me no credit; neither did my mom, nor Trey. They all thought I was this high maintenance spoiled brat.

In some cases, I knew I was wrong, and in this case, I was dead wrong. I was dating a much older guy named Sam. He looked real good to be thirty-one years old. He wasn't the richest guy I've dated, but he was what you would call living comfortable. He had a good corporate job. He had a pretty decent salary. He made over six figures a year. He invested his money by buying stocks and bonds and mutual funds. He had a few cars and a nice-sized home. But he also came with a nice-sized problem: a wife.

Sam and I were in love. I knew it would never really work out. I knew deep down in my heart that he wouldn't leave his family to be with me. I tried not to get myself so wrapped up into him.

Sam wanted to see me when I got out of school. I knew that I was on probation with moms, but I had to go see him. We were spending less time together because his wife had been nagging him so much. I think she started to catch on to the fact that he was seeing another woman but she hadn't actually caught us in action.

I left school a bit early to meet up with him. It took me twenty minutes to drive to the hotel where we met. Sam always tried his best to make things special for me. I guess he felt bad because he couldn't give me more of his time. As soon as I made it up to the suite he grabbed me and started kissing my neck while he unbuttoned my shirt.

"Damn baby, can I get in the door good enough?"

"I missed you, I haven't seen you in about three weeks. I couldn't wait to get my hands on you. I have been fantasizing about this all week."

He started to take every piece of my clothing off. When he entered me I felt relieved. I needed this from him just as much as he needed it from me. We were both so wrapped up in our moment that we didn't care about anything. His phone was ringing off the hook and I knew that I was due at home right now. We didn't care; we kept on going. If Mom was going to put me on punishment again, it would be well worth it. I barely got to see him.

After we were done I laid in his arms.

"I didn't realize how much I missed you. That felt so good it almost made me forget to ask you about this guy named Trey. I heard that whenever you're around him you become flirty with him. What's up with that? Ain't you supposed to be my woman?"

"Where did you hear that from?" I asked with a confused look on my face. I was trying to figure out who could be the snitch.

"That's all you could say?" He looked like he would explode at any moment.

"What do you care? You have a whole family at home. I get put on the back burner for them all the time. I see you like once a week if I'm lucky, and you have the nerve to be in my face about flirting with another man."

"You damn right. I sacrifice everything for you. I get you whatever you want. I spend more money on you than both my wife and my child. Things are different between my wife and me. We haven't been intimate in months. My dick won't even get hard around her anymore."

We'd done this same conversation a thousand times and it always led up to me asking him the same thing.

"So when are you leaving her?"

This is the question that he hated for me to ask but I hated having to ask him as well. Now he really had an angry look on his face.

"I know you hate when I bring that subject up, but I think you need to hear it. You got me hanging on by a string for the last year in a half and I'm tired.

I think this relationship is making me crazy." I flopped down on the bed and started to cry.

He then felt bad for me so he hugged me as tight as he could.

"I'm sorry, I didn't expect for things to turn out the way they have but it's hard to break it off with my wife. She's going to through something and I will feel awful if I left her right now."

"But there's no sense in leading her on. She's going to be more hurt."

He sat there for a moment and thought about it all. "I'll think of something," he said as he zipped up his pants.

I looked him dead in his face and told him just like this: "You know I've heard this over a million times. If you don't make some type of move and I mean quick, I'm moving on with my life."

I walked out the door and into my car. I drove home with a lot on my mind. I was in love with a person I knew I could not be with. This relationship was so unhealthy and toxic, but we couldn't just let things go. Whenever I saw him we would have a great time but our conversations always led up to the same argument.

When I got home the coast was clear. My mom hadn't come home yet. I went up stairs to my room and my cell phone rang; it was my girl Katrina.

"Hey girl what's up with you?" she asked.

"I saw Sam and we had great sex then we got into another argument again."

"About the same shit?"

"Yes, and I guess someone supposedly told Sam that I been flirting with Trey."

"Who do you think it could be?"

"Some loser who probably tried to get at me and I turned him down, but anyway, Sam somehow feels like he has the right to get mad at me when he's sleeping with another woman every night. And he have the nerves to say he's not fucking her."

"You believe him?"

"Hell no, I don't believe him! He is a freaking man for crying out loud. Besides who cares if he cops an attitude, he's not fully committing himself, so why should I? Anyway, enough about me and my man problems, what's going on with you?"

"Well my grades are horrible and my supposed boyfriend Marcus ain't called me in a week."

"He's cheating then. A whole week? Come on now," I reminded her.

"It *could* be something else. You don't give a nigga any slack, huh

"Hell no, and whatever drama he throws your way, don't believe his ass. Alright girl, I'll talk to you tomorrow."

I looked out the window and I saw my mom's car pulling in the driveway. I hurried up and changed out of my clothes and into some sweats and a t-shirt. I pulled out my books and sat at my desk.

When Mom's saw me, she looked impressed.

"You doing homework?" she asked with a surprised look on her face." Sabrina told me you were looking for a college to go to. I am very proud of you, keep up the good work and I will take you off restriction in a few days."

That was music to my ears.

When I got to school the next day I saw my girls Carmen and Katrina out in the front waiting for me.

"Still seeing that married man." said Carmen.

"How you know?"

She glanced over at Katrina.

"I'm sorry," said Katrina. "I thought we were all friends."

"Yeah," said Carmen." I thought we were all friends."

"Yeah but look at the negative input you have on the situation. You had to bring up the fact that he was married like I forgot about it or something."

"Oh, I'm sorry; did I hit a sensitive spot?"

"Okay, that's enough Carmen," said Katrina.

"Well that's the reason why I don't tell you anything now." I wasn't going to let Carmen get to me. She was probably upset with her boyfriend so she wanted me to join her club but it wasn't going to happen.

CHAPTER 3

Busted

When I got home Sabrina was sitting on the sofa.

"What are you doing here?" I asked.

"I was actually waiting for you to come home."

"Why?"

"Mom told me you're on restriction. That means coming straight home from school. But I hear the other day you were spotted with this older guy named Sam."

"How?" I asked her.

"Someone I know spotted you. She saw you two together."

"You're not going to tell Mom are you? You are supposed to be my best friend," I reminded her.

"I'm not going to be a snitch, but you have to stop seeing that guy. He's too old for you. He could go down for statutory rape, and I hear that he's married."

"For real, he's married?" I acted surprised. I had to act as if I didn't know. I couldn't let my goodie-two-shoes sister know that I knew.

"Since he's married and is a decade and four years you're senior, I would advise you to never see him again."

For the rest of the day I was irritated. I had a million and one thoughts running through my head. I was really upset because now my sister was going to be all in my business. Bad enough we already had a hard time seeing each other. Now things were going to get even more complicated.

The next morning my mom took me off punishment. I wanted to go out and celebrate, maybe even have a cocktail or two. I asked the girls to join me and we decided to go to the pool hall. It was where most kids our age hung out. They served alcohol, but we weren't allowed to drink any of it. But the girls and I had different plans: we always had an older person buy our alcohol from the corner store. We bought sixteen-ounce juice bottles. We would pour half the juice out and fill the rest with alcohol. The working staff never knew that we were drinking.

As soon we walked inside, I spotted Trey. I went over to talk to him.

"Hey sexy, how are you?" I whispered in his ear.

"I'm good Miss Lady, and how are you?"

"Be better if I had you," I said with a big smile on my face.

"I bet," he said as he kept on playing his game of pool.

"Why don't you like me?" I yelled at him.

"You got life all twisted, and you're a teenager. I did a bunch of stupid shit when I was young so I guess that means you're a normal teen. "As he was talking he made no eye contact with me what so ever. He kept his eyes on the game.

"So what I got to do to get you? I've been having a crush on you for years."

"Cristina, you're seventeen years old, that means you're jailbait."

"Come on now, who really follows that?"

"I do," he said as he concentrated on his game.

"You would," I said as I walked away.

I went over to my girls. It was my turn to play Carmen because Katrina had lost. In the middle of our game I spotted Chris. The guy that I met the other day at the mall. He and two of his friends came walking through the door.

They headed straight for the bar. When Chris noticed me, his face lit up.

"Hey man, get my drink for me," he said as he gave his boy a twenty-dollar bill. Then he made his way toward me.

"Hey baby you looking real lovely."

"Thanks, you're looking nice yourself," I told him as I checked him out from head to toe.

"How come you didn't give a brother a call? I've been waiting for that call."

"Really," I said, smiling at him.

He signaled for his friends to come over to our section.

"Can I get you ladies any drinks?" asked Chris.

"Were not old enough," said Katrina.

"We have some liquor in these cranberry juice bottles," I added.

"I remember those days," said Chris.

"Well since Chris is being rude, my name is Kayden and this is my boy Max."

"The three of us own this joint," added Chris.

"Really?" asked Carmen.

Katrina and I both were skeptical. We looked at each other and we both had that look on our face, the look that meant we weren't buying it.

"No, really," said Kayden. He had his eyes on Carmen. She had her eyes set on him also.

"What are you ladies having? We got y'all, it's all good," said Max.

"How about three Mai-Tais?" said Katrina?

"What y'all know about that?" asked Kayden.

"We know a lil sumtin' sumtin," I added.

Chris and I sat down while Max went to get our drinks.

"So where's your man?" was the first thing that came out of
Chris mouth.

"My situation is sort of confusing, I'm with someone, but then
I'm not. He's married and he's supposed to be leaving his wife but
I don't know if that will ever happen. And he doesn't want me
associating with other guys."

He gave me a weird look.

"I know it sounds confusing and I really love him.

"Well I say get rid of the loser and get with a winner. I got
everything you would want or need. This ain't my only business baby
girl. I got a car lot, a club, and my own clothing line. I got so many
things lined up its ridiculous."

"You sure do know how to sell yourself," I laughed.

"Are you guys sure this is okay? Nobody's going to get in any
trouble because of us drinking in here, right?" Katrina asked.

"Nah, it's cool we run this joint and what we say goes," said
Kayden.

Everything was going great and everyone was having a good
time. Then I noticed Trey kept looking our way and was whispering
to his friend. Next thing I knew Trey was calling me over to his
table.

"Is everything okay?" I asked him.

"Where do you know that guy from and why does he have you
drinking liquor? You guys are minors; you're not even old enough
to buy cigarettes."

"His name is Chris, I met him at the mall and he's the owner of
this pool hall and why are you all of a sudden worried about me?"

"I'm trying to keep an eye on you, that's all. I am your sister's
husband friend. And somebody needs to keep an eye on you because
you're getting out of control young lady."

"Where do you get off judging me?"

"Look, I'm not about to get into this with you all I know is that you and your friends need to put away those drinks or I will be forced to embarrass you."

"You wouldn't."

"I sure would," he said without hesitation.

"It wouldn't benefit you any, so why don't you just leave me alone. You don't want me no way."

"That's not what this is about. I know them cats and they aren't really that cool from what I know. Just tell them that you can't drink anymore or I will be forced to handle the situation."

"Whatever," I said and walked away. I wasn't worried about what he was saying; he needed to calm down. I went back over to our table. I gave Chris a hug and we continued to watch Kayden and Carmen play pool. Katrina and Max were having a conversation of their own.

"Are you ladies enjoying yourselves?" asked Chris.

"Yes," Katrina and I answered.

"Can I get you another round of drinks?" asked Chris.

"Nah, that's okay," I said, trying to avoid the drama because I could see Trey watching my every move from the corner of his eye. I must admit I did enjoy watching him get so angry over me but I didn't want him and Chris to start fighting.

"Get these ladies one more round," Chris told the cocktail waitress.

"No thanks, we're good," I told him.

"What you talking about? I want another drink," blurted out Katrina.

"Come on, have one more. I'll make sure you get home safely."

Next thing I knew, Trey came out of nowhere.

"Didn't she say no?"

"Man, don't come at me with that corny ass shit," said Chris.

"She said no. Look, I know who you guys are. These girl's are only seventeen. I'm sure you already knew that, but you don't care," Trey said as he came towards Chris.

"Why you all up in mines? Trying to be Mr. Captain, save a hoe ass motherfucker!"

"You both need to calm down." I jumped in the middle.

"Let them fight," yelled Carmen.

"Trey, it's not a big deal," I tried to convince him.

"You don't have to say nothing to him. I'm going to whoop his ass in about three seconds," said Chris.

I finally pulled them apart. "Wait a minute, Please stop, for me." I looked Chris in his eyes and he instantly sat back down.

"You lucky I like her, else I would have whooped your ass."

"And after I beat the shit out of you, I'd get this little pool hall closed down for giving minors alcohol. Come on girls, I'm taking y'all home right now."

"But Trey," I mumbled.

"Not another word or I will call your sister and she will call your mom and I know you don't want that." He was dead serious.

I looked at the girls and signaled for us to leave. Chris read my lips as I mouthed the words "Call you later!"

Chris nodded his head and I gave him a smile.

He smiled back at me and I read his lips that said "You better!"

When we got inside Trey's brand new black Denali truck with twenty-two inch rims, I sat in the front while the girls sat in the back.

"Do you know what you girls were getting yourselves into?" he asked.

"Some free drinks," I blurted out, the girls and me started laughing.

"See, that's what I'm talking about," he said as he kept his eyes on the road. You girls don't have a clue, he said ask he shook his head.

He dropped the girls off and now it was just him and I alone in his car.

For a while there was dead silence. I watched Trey pay attention to the road. I guess he was done talking to me, I guessed he figured I was hopeless and it was no use teaching me anything.

"Now I know you have some type of feelings for me," I said. "You couldn't stand another man all over me."

"Girl, please!" he said as he kept paying attention to the road.

"Admit it," I said as I went to kiss his neck.

He immediately pulled the car over. "Look, I am trying to drive. I am trying to do you a favor. If I wasn't around, Lord only knows what would happen to you. You would have either gone home with that dude or you would have driven your car drunk with your friends inside. You could have gotten yourself in a car- wreck or even gotten a DUI and, you're only seventeen."

We pulled up in front of my house.

"Can you come get me in the morning so that I can get my car?" I asked him as I gave him my sad little girl face.

"Yeah," he said blankly. "One more thing, I don't want you to ever see that guy again."

"Why not?"

"He's bad news, and are you really asking that right now?"

"Alright, I won't see him" I went inside and went to bed.

School was boring as usual. When lunchtime came around, I couldn't take it anymore. I grabbed my cell phone from my purse and I went through it to see who I could call. I tried calling Sam but I got his voicemail. I was a little sad that I couldn't even spend time with him when I wanted. I couldn't even call him if I needed someone to talk to. And what my sister told me about him stayed on my mind. I thought about calling Chris, but what Trey told me kept running through my mind: *He's bad news.* But there was something about him that made me want to get to know more of him. He seemed like a free spirit that just did what he wanted. When he wanted and with whom he wanted. He was tempting. So I decided to give him a call anyway.

"Hello?" he said in an aggravated voice.

"Is this Chris?" I asked.

"Yeah, you called my phone didn't you?"

"Yeah but I thought—"

Before I could finish speaking he cut me off.

"Man who is this? I got things to do."

"Cristina, remember me from the pool hall?"

"Oh yeah," he said as his tone of voice changed. "Hey girl, why are you just now calling? It's been weeks."

"I've been sort of busy."

"So you are just Miss Important?"

"No, I just been busy concentrating on school and all."

"That guy didn't tell your moms on you or anything like that, did he?"

"No, he just gave me the underage drinking lecture as if I hadn't heard it a Thousand times."

"I hate it when people get all up in other people's shit. That dude really needed to mind his business that night. He almost had got his head busted in."

"Let's talk less about him and more about you." I said, changing the subject.

"I'm twenty nine and I'm all about business. I don't have time for games. I'm looking for a down ass chic. I can tell you more about me in person, what's up with lunch?"

"That sounds good I'm starving."

"Meet me at Pat's in about twenty minutes," he said and he hung up.

I drove to Pat's Diner and I was there in twenty minutes exactly. I looked inside for him and he wasn't there. I sat down at a table for two. The waitress came over."Can I get you anything?"

"I'll start out with some water"

"Okay," she said as she gave me a smile. She was not only beautiful but she was also very polite.

Ten minutes went by and I was sipping water all by myself. I signaled for the waitress to come over again. "Can I order a salad with cheese sprinkled over the top please?"

"Sure, but why are you over here sitting by yourself?"

"My date is late." I felt embarrassed.

I kept looking at my watch. I called his phone but the answering machine came on the first ring. A few minutes went by and my salad came. I told myself if he wasn't here by the time I was finished with my salad, I was gone. I got down to the last bite and then he came walking in the diner like he was the coolest thing in the town.

"Hey baby how you doing?" He kissed my cheek and then he sat down. "Sorry I'm late."

"Well, I almost left, you came just in time.

"This dude who was handling some business for me just messed up, I'm sorry." "A phone call would have been nice, a text or something saying that you were running late."

"I apologize once more. I will make it up to you, I promise."

We ordered our food then we chatted.

"So what is it exactly that you do?" I asked him.

"Well my business partners and I own that pool hall and I own a night club and a car lot. I've got a clothing line coming out. I own a few properties. Plus we've got our own company that involves the entertainment industry."

"What kind of entertainment?"

"You watch music videos?"

"Of course, why?"

"Because the girls in them come through us. We audition them, they get paid, and that's how it works."

"Really? I always wanted to become famous."

"Well maybe I could get you a lead role in a music video."

"Really?" I asked. This sounded too good to be true.

"You got the look, that's for sure."

Now he had my full attention.

"So what are your goals in life?" he asked me.

"I basically want to be in the entertainment field."

"What is it that you want to do in the entertainment industry?"

"I don't know. Maybe become a singer or a dancer. Maybe even an actress or a model. Who knows? All I know is that I want to be in the spotlight. But my sister and my mom have different plans for me. They have all the money I need for school just waiting for me. I just don't think college is for everyone."

"So you think you got what it takes to for Hollywood huh?"

"Yeah I do, I got the personality, the look, and most def the body to go with it all."

"You're Miss Sure about yourself, huh?"

"Gotta have confidence."

"You seem like a cool person. I can understand you got a man and all, but I would like to keep a cool, friendly or maybe even a business relationship with you."

"Sounds good to me," I agreed.

"So, I got to go and head out to this business meeting. I will catch back up with you later." He left enough money for the bill and the waitress a good tip.

As I was getting up to leave the waitress approached me.

"I didn't mean to be all up in your conversation but did he say he could get you in music videos?"

"Yeah."

"I always wanted to be in a music video. If I wrote down my number would you give it to him?"

She did look pretty enough to be on TV. "Sure, what's your name?"

"Sharon," she said as she wrote down her phone number.

I couldn't shake the thought that I looked a lot like her. "Okay I will give it to him."

"Thanks so much," she said with an excited look on her face.

When I got home my sister was in the living room waiting

for me. She was the last person I wanted to see. All she was good for these days was getting on my back. I felt like she was trying to control my life.

"So Chrissie, what are you going to do about school? You will be graduating in a few months and you need to decide on a college."

"I've decided to go to a community college first."

"Not a university?"

"I'm just not ready for the hype yet."

"I'm disappointed in you." She got up to leave.

"I know you care and all, but it's my life and you can't control everything."

I went upstairs. I felt bad but at the same time I felt some sense of relief. I had finally stood up to my controlling sister.

It was over two weeks and I still hadn't heard from Sam. I had been checking my phone every ten seconds. But to keep myself occupied, I was hanging around Chris. We were becoming good friends. He booked me for a video shoot that was coming up and I was nervous but excited at the same time.

When I told my friends Katrina and Carmen they didn't seem too thrilled.

They were probably just jealous because they weren't going to be in the video. I didn't care one way or another. I was following my dream.

The morning of the shoot I was nervous out of my mind. I had about three outfits lined up for the event. I had an all-black Victoria's secret bikini and a black mini with some black heels. I also had a mini dress with long sleeves that hung under the shoulders and I had some short shorts with a tube top. I was a hot mamma.

It was a Saturday morning. I had to get up two hours earlier than usual. I almost didn't get up but I kept telling myself this was my dream. Somehow I dragged myself out of the bed.

I showed up to the video shoot in some sweatpants and with my hair in rollers. Out of the thirteen girls that were here only about three of us were actually cute. Most of these girls were very superficial. Everything from their nails and hair, eyelashes, boobs, jewelry and clothes. Too many fake things at once just weren't a good look.

I spotted the waitress that I met the other day. She walked up to me.

"I see you made it up here."

"Yeah it was hard, but I made it."

"I think we're the two prettiest ones," she said as she laughed.

"I know right? I've seen some Giga pets up in here." We both laughed.

"So how old are you?" I asked her.

"I'm twenty two. How old are you?"

"I'm seventeen"

"Seriously? I thought you were much older, not` that you look it, it's just that you Seem really mature and smart."

"Well, thanks."

We were on scene two, the scene had two girls in a hot tub with one of the rappers Two girls who came earlier already claimed the scene. Which was fine; I wasn't tripping on being all up in the camera like these other chicks were. I knew that I would stand out.

The two girls were positioned in the tub and the rapper sat in the middle of them. They shot the scene a few times. All of a sudden, he looked at them both from left to right and got up. Everyone was trying to figure out what he was doing.

He looked at all the girls and then he said, "I'm not trying to be rude or disrespectful but I want the twins in my scene." He pointed directly at us.

Oh now some shit's about to jump off, was the first thing I thought. But then I was like it's his video, his call. The ladies stepped out of the tub and we took their places.

"We're not twins. We barely know each other."

"Yeah, we just met the other day," she added.

He poured three glasses of champagne and we started shooting the scene. I could see this dude was attracted to me; he was all over me as we were shooting. After the scene was completed I went to change outfits. The girl who got booted off the set came inside the bathroom. She looked me up and down and said, "You know he already tried to get with me."

"Okay," was all I said. She looked confused.

"He ain't even got that much money."

"Okay, I heard ya," I said and walked out the door. Bitches ain't got no life, I thought.

For the rest of the day the bitch kept throwing these salty looks at me. That rapper did try to give me his number but I didn't want it; after all he did try to flirt with almost every girl in there. After the video shoot was all said and done, Sharon and I decided to grab a bite to eat.

When Sharon saw my car she was amazed.

"Oh my goodness, girl, I didn't know you was rolling like that! What model is this?"

"This is the S430. But wait till my graduation I'm a get a sl550."

"So you are you going to trade this one in?"

"Hell no, this is my first baby. I can't do that," I explained to her.

"So, are your parents rich or something?"

"Naw, my mom's middleclass. She works and makes a decent salary. My father passed away and I inherited a good amount of money from him."

When we got inside the restaurant I received a call from Chris.

"How did the shoot go?" he asked.

"It went pretty well, except for the girls trying to hate. You know how that goes."

"As good as you look you're going to have that problem all the time. Did Sharon go to the shoot?" he asked.

"Yeah, as a matter of fact she's sitting here now."

"Okay great, so do you have plans for this weekend?" he asked.

"No," I answered.

"Well I'm supposed to be going to Vegas for the weekend and I wanted to know if you wanted to join me."

I thought about it for a second. "My mom would never let me and besides I don't have an I.D."

"You can use my I.D," Sharon butted in. "You can pass for me."

"You would do that?" I asked her.

"Sure, no problem."

"You're a lifesaver."

"What are you going to tell your mom?"

"I could tell her anything. The problem is my sister. I can't just tell her anything."

"You have an older sister?"

"Yes and she practically raised me so she sometimes get carried away and she thinks she's my mom. But I will figure something out somehow."

CHAPTER 4

Going to Vegas

Friday night was the night we were leaving. I had Sharon's I.D and the perfect excuse for my mom, I was ready. The best news was that Sabrina was gone with her husband Jay. They skipped out of town on a small romantic getaway, which they did a lot, and they left their child with my mom.

We were only going to be gone for the weekend, but I packed like I was going to be gone for a month. I had five pairs of shoes, seven shirts, two pairs of jeans, three dresses, and two skirts, not to mention my cosmetics and jewelry. I had my bags all ready to go. I told mom that I was going to Katrina's house for the weekend.

Katrina begged to borrow my car since I was going to be leaving it at her house. I agreed since she was doing a favor for me. She always covered for me.

When the cab arrived I hugged Katrina and I handed over my keys.

"Be careful and call me if you need me, She said."

I had knots in my stomach. I was wild and bold but I think this was going to top it all. I was going to Sin City for the first time and yet I was way underage and I was with a guy I barely even knew.

When I got to the airport I spotted Chris. We checked in all of our luggage and next thing I knew we were flying first class to Vegas.

When we arrived I was amazed by how the city was lit up. There were people everywhere and lights all around; Vegas had so much going on. I had money an I.D that said I was over twenty-one. My hair was banging I had some fly clothes to wear, I was ready to dive in.

Chris was happy because he could see in my eyes how excited I was. We got in the cab and we left the airport, we pulled up to a nice sized home in a nice and quiet neighborhood.

Is this your house? " I asked.

"Yeah this is my house, girl." He said it as if I was already supposed to know. It was a beautiful four bedroom two-and-a-half bathrooms home. I wondered why he needed all the space unless he had a family.

"This is just an extra house for me since I come out here on a regular basis. Sometimes my boys come and crash in it when they're out here visiting."

I walked around checking out the house. It was pretty lavish. Not bad, not bad at all, I thought to myself.

To my surprise there was a woman lying on the couch with a pink extra short silk nightgown. She looked like she was Latina. Her hair was brown and blonde and she had it pinned up. She was on the phone and she was talking loudly.

"Who's that?" I asked.

"Oh that's Veronica. She's just the girl that has been down with me from day one. She handles business for me.

"Is she your girlfriend?" I asked out of curiosity.

"No way, she wants a brother and all but she's just not for me." He showed me to my guest room and told me to be ready in an hour.

"Where are we going?" I asked.

"Veronica's going to take you out to the Vegas strip."

"You're not coming with us?" I asked.

"No, I got to handle some business."

I was ready to head out but I wasn't so excited about going with Veronica. I didn't like her personality already, just from observing her. She was loud and I hated loud people, especially loud females.

I went inside my suitcase to look for something grown and sexy. I had to make sure I looked over twenty-one. I didn't want those people carding me over a hundred times. One hour later I was almost ready to go and I was looking sexier than ever.

I then heard a loud voice. "Are you ready yet?"

"In like, two minutes," I yelled back. I wondered why she couldn't just knock on the door and ask me if I was ready. She had to yell it out. I knew that I wasn't going to vibe with her.

When I came out, Chris had his eyes on my breasts. "Those look good, I mean you look good," he laughed.

"You meant what you was about to say the first time," I said as I laughed.

Now Veronica looked like she was getting agitated.

It didn't take a psychic to see that she had feelings for Chris.

"Alright, we better get headed out before it becomes too late," said Veronica. We hopped in the silver drop top Mercedes and were on our way to the strip.

The car was dead silent until Veronica opened her mouth. "So Cristina, how old are you?" she asked.

I hated when this was the first question that came out of an older woman's mouth, especially the way she said it like she knew I was young.

"I'm seventeen, a mature seventeen."

"Well damn girl, what's with the attitude? I never said that you were immature."

"The way you came off sound that way."

"Chris always brings around young girls, that's all."

Now I knew that she was really trying her best to get under my skin, but I wasn't going to let her. "Well that's good for him," I said and I then turned on the radio.

"Where are we going any way?" I asked.

"To a club," she answered. "And did you even bring an I.D.?"

"Of course."

"Well good, because you're going to need it."

"How old are you?" I asked her with attitude.

"Twenty-three," she answered.

This bitch was pretty young herself. The way she walked, the way she talked, the way she moved, I thought she was at least thirty. I knew she was trying to be funny but she didn't know who she was fucking with. I was young but I was sharp-witted and I was always quick to snap back on a Bitch.

The club was upscale and classy. Not the kind of clubs I was used to seeing around my neck of the woods. Veronica headed for the bathroom and I headed straight to the bar. I ordered a Long Island Iced Tea, something I knew that was going to get me drunk. I sat at the bar, watching everyone get they're party on. Veronica spotted me and came my way.

"Cristina, I got a call so I got to make a quick run. I should only be gone for an hour."

"So you mean to tell me you leaving in this club by myself? You act like I've been in Vegas before."

"Come here; Let me introduce you to a couple of people so you won't feel alone."

I'd just arrived to this town and suddenly I was getting passed around from stranger to stranger.

"This is Tommy the bartender and this is Teddy the bouncer. I'll be back in an hour."

I looked confused, but I agreed, Besides, Tommy and Teddy seemed pretty cool.

"So where are you from?" asked Teddy.

"The Bay Area."

"What part of the Bay Area?" he asked.

"San Francisco," I answered. I was finished with my drink already.

"Damn girl, you drank that pretty fast," said Tommy.

"Can I have one more?" I asked.

Next thing you know I was feeling my alcohol and I was starting to get worried because a whole hour had gone by and still no Veronica. This was not how I planned on spending my first trip to Sin City, alone talking to two strangers. I was starting to panic but I told myself to relax.

Since I was in Vegas I decided to make the most of my trip. I decided to mingle in with the crowd. I heard a song I liked and started dancing. I was just starting to get into my groove when a man and woman approached me. She looked really exotic like she was some type of dancer or entertainer. Her breasts were definitely silicone. Her hair was platinum blonde and she had on a real short dress with eight inch heels. She pulled me aside and she touched my hair.

"Is this all your hair?" she asked.

"Yeah?" I said in a confused voice.

"It's pretty and so are you," she said, as she looked me up and down as if she wanted to eat me. "Let me just get down to the point: my guy friend likes you. He wanted me to ask you what you do for a living, I have a proposition for you if you want to make a whole lot of money, and I strongly believe you got what it takes."

I didn't know what she was talking about. It sounded like she was trying to run some serious game on me. She handed me a card and I placed it in my pocket.

"Think about it and give me a call," she said as she walked away.

I looked at my watch. Another thirty minutes had gone by and now I was starting to panic. I started looking around in the crowd, still no Veronica. I didn't have her cell phone number so I called

Chris. I explained to him how Veronica told me she would be back in an hour and it was now two hours.

He told me not to panic and that he would come get me. I sat at the bar and I worked on my fourth drink. I then went to the restroom and as soon as I came out, I saw her.

"Why in the hell would you leave me at this club all by myself for two whole hours?" I yelled.

"I was handling some important business," she said in a nasty voice. "Did you call Chris?"

"Yeah, I don't know you, I barely know him and I'm in some town I don't know."

"Why did you call him? Now I got to hear his mouth."

On the way back home we were quiet. I could tell she got really pissed off when I told her that I called Chris.

When we got to the house Chris was waiting in the front room for us. He seemed quite upset too.

"What did I tell you?" He yelled to Veronica. "I told you not to handle any business. I told you not to leave her side and instead you did the exact opposite."

"I'm sorry, I didn't mean to," was all she got a chance to blurt out.

He finished with "Go to your room."

I stood there in shock, even more confused about their relationship.

I barely got any sleep. That whole situation was weird. I wondered why he was treating her like a child. I wanted to ask him but I guess it was none of my business. I wasn't his girl and he knew I was seeing someone else. I felt uncomfortable and I wanted to go home.

Early in the morning, around seven, Chris came into my room. I was already awake.

He greeted me with a kiss on my forehead. "I'm sorry about last night. I specifically told Veronica not to leave you. I know that you're having a bad time but I promise I will make it up to you. Today is a brand new day and we are going to spend it together," he said with a smile. I wasn't too thrilled. I thought he was full of shit and I wanted to go home.

"So what are we doing?" I asked him in a dry voice.

"We are first going out to breakfast."

I hopped out of the bed right away because breakfast sounded good. I got dressed and we headed out to a breakfast spot. After we were done eating, he took me shopping for a couple of outfits. After shopping we decided to go out for massages. Later on that night we went out to dinner and we enjoyed a movie. The day was much better. No Veronica in sight.

As soon as my airplane landed I called Katrina so that she could pick me up from the airport. I tried calling her a few times but she wasn't picking up her phone. I was really pissed off because I was tired, I was due at home and besides she had my car. I was frustrated after thirty minutes went by, I decided to catch a cab to her house and get my car myself.

When I got there, I saw my car all wrecked up.

"My baby," I cried. I recognized it by the license plate. I was blown away. I knocked on the door and Katrina opened it. She had the dumbest look on her face when she saw me.

"Why haven't you been answering my phone calls?" I yelled out.

"I'm so sorry, Cristina I just didn't know what to say. It was an accident."

I was so angry I wanted to just haul off and hit her.

"You shouldn't be that mad. I know you have full coverage insurance."

"So what the fuck does that mean? You can just wreck my car because I have insurance. Are you going to pay the deductible?"

"Come on Cristina, you got the money, why are you acting like that?"

I was so angry that I just punched her dead in her face.

She was in shock as she wiped the blood off of her mouth. She punched me back and before I knew it, I was having a fistfight with one of my best friends. We were rumbling all over her living room.

Her brother finally pulled us apart.

"You're just a bitch Cristina, all you do is think about yourself. You have never been my real friend."

"Well bitch, you just been jealous of me anyway. You just mad because your hair won't grow past your neck and I look way better. I know it just pisses you off that all the guys' want me, not you or Carmen."

"Well bitch that's why Sam ain't never gonna leave his wife for you and Trey ain't never gonna want you."

"You ole raggedy broke bitch, you can't even get no money out of any of these dudes you're fucking, you just a broke hoe," I yelled as I tried to reach over her brother to get one last hit in. "At least Sam gives me money and I'm about to get a way better Benz than that anyway!"

"Shorty you got to leave," her brother said as he handed me my things. I walked out the house and I slammed the door. I was not only angry by the fact that she crashed my car but she had a messed up way of thinking, just like everyone else did. Just because I had a few dollars in the bank, that did not make me rich. She should pay for her own mistakes. She was flat out wrong.

My car wasn't moving so I had to walk home and had to think of some type of lie to tell my mom. When I made it home I was scared out of my mind. I could hear my heart pounding right when I saw her car sitting outside. I took a deep breath and walked in the house. I saw moms on the couch reading the newspaper.

"Mom, I have some bad news," I blurted out.

"What is it now Cristina?" she asked.

"I got into a car accident, but I'm fine."

"Where's your car?" she asked, in a calm voice.

"It's parked at Katrina's house but I've arranged for the tow truck to pick it up."

"You know, you're starting to become a good liar, Cristina. There was an accident in your car, but I know for a fact that you were nowhere near your car at the time, so who was driving?"

"It happened when I got sick and Katrina went to the store to get me some medicine," I explained.

"Katrina wasn't even driving, some guy was. Your sister's husband Jay just happened to be riding by the scene of the accident and saw some boy was driving. Jay noticed your car and the license plate and checked out the scene. Katrina and you were nowhere to be found."

I couldn't speak or move. I was humiliated by the fact that I was being exposed as a liar but even more so by the fact that Katrina had let her boyfriend drive my car.

"Mom, I swear I didn't have any clue some guy was driving my car. Katrina must have let her boyfriend drive it when I sleep or something. I stayed in the house the whole time because I didn't feel well."

"That's mighty funny because I called over to Katrina's house several times and she had every excuse why you weren't there, and I called your phone several times but it just kept sending me to voicemail."

I had never been caught in a lie this big with my mom.

"You're on a huge punishment. Go upstairs and think about how you're going to be without a car since you want to let your friends borrow it, and I'm taking your phone since you don't know how to answer it."

I ran up the stairs and yelled from the top. "I'm going to be eighteen soon and I want all my money out of the account, and I'm moving the hell out of this place. I hate you, I hate Sabrina and I hate that snitch Jay and I hate Katrina. I went inside my room and slammed the door shut and I got inside my bed. Huge watermelon tears ran down my cheeks. I was pissed off at everyone. I didn't know how I would manage without a car or a phone. My life was over.

CHAPTER 5

A New Car

*A*fter missing a few days of school, my mom made me go back. I was devastated going to school with no car or phone. I was especially embarrassed to let Katrina and Carmen see me with no phone or car especially since I'd bragged that I was getting a brand new car. When I got to school it was kind of cool to see that everyone had missed me. All the guys were hugging me and about three guys asked me on a lunch date. I decided to go out with James Townsend, Katrina's crush. I chose him just to piss her off.

When lunchtime came around Katrina got a glimpse of us pulling off in his white BMW. The look on her face was priceless and I knew she was heated. When we got back to school I could hear all the talk. Already there were rumors being spread about me and James being an item.

After school I was embarrassed. I was used to driving out of the school's parking lot with the hottest car. I asked James to give me a ride home, but he couldn't because he had basketball practice. I wanted to call a taxi or someone to come and pick me up, but I had no phone.

I knew it wouldn't be easy but I took a deep breath and I started my walk home. I was doing good, making sure no spotted me walking up until Dianna and Carmen and Katrina pulled alongside of me.

"Where's your car?" blurted out Carmen as she laughed.

"Where's your hot lunch date?" asked Katrina.

"Look at the princess walking home," said Carmen and then they all laughed in unison.

"My car is in the shop, you Bitches. You're gonna see, I'm going to be the baddest bitch up at the school once again," I yelled.

"Yeah, but right now you're walking" said Katrina as they drove off.

I was so humiliated.

The next day it was time for me to go to school but I decided that I wasn't going to go. I was way too proud to be going to school with no car or phone. I had an image to maintain and walking to school wasn't going to cut it. I got dressed as usual and left at my normal time. I went to the payphone to call up Sharon to see if I could duck down in her place until school let out. Sharon said it was cool. So for the next couple weeks I awoke around my usual time and I pretended as if I was going to school every morning. I still was trying to get a hold of Sam and this time, to my surprise, he answered.

"I've been trying to reach you for so long, Sam! So much has happened," I told him.

"My wife has been getting suspicious, she's been going through my phone, smelling my clothes when I come home, and calling me ten times a day. She knows something is up."

"Well I need you too, and I feel like you are putting her needs and wants before me and you keep promising me that you will be with me."

"Baby calm down, I just need more time, you know you're the one I'm going to end up with eventually"

"You want me to calm down? I have no car or cell phone right now. I'm on a huge punishment, nothing is going right for me right now."

"Wow, what happened?" he asked.

"She found out I had been skipping school for a couple of weeks straight."

I lied, I couldn't tell Sam that I was out in Las Vegas with Chris and that I caught in a huge lie with Moms.

"I'm so sorry baby; I didn't know you were going through all of that. Don't worry, Daddy's here to take care of you, I'm going to get you a new car and a phone first thing tomorrow morning."

"You're the best, I love you!"

"I love you too sweetheart, so hold tight until tomorrow."

That night I went to sleep with a sense of relief; Sam was going to take care of everything.

The next morning I met Sam at the doughnut shop bright and early just like he instructed. I ordered a glazed doughnut, which was my favorite, and a cup of hot chocolate. I was a bit nervous by the fact that I hadn't seen him in almost a month.

"Hey, baby I missed you so much," Sam said as he kissed my face.

"Alright Cristina, this is an early birthday present, you ready to go car shopping?"

"Hell yeah, I can't wait. Being a few weeks without a car is hell and I don't know how people do it."

When we got to the dealers, I picked out a white s1550 Mercedes Benz.

"You would get the most extravagant car in the whole entire lot," said Sam as he laughed and wrote a check for the down payment and agreed to pay the rest in installments.

"I know I'm gonna be getting me some pussy today with all this damn money I just spent."

"Don't worry, I got you." I told him. I could see in his eyes that he was anxious to get some of me especially since it'd been so long.

But he had no idea how badly I wanted him, so the feeling was mutual.

I examined my new car thoroughly. I grew even more excited as I looked at all the new features that my old car didn't have.

"You're the best," I told him as I hugged him once more. I couldn't wait to see the look on those hoe's faces when I showed up at the school with this car. A girl like me will always come out on top.

I was in a good mood the next morning and I couldn't wait to go to school. If those hoes thought it was over for me, they had another thought coming. I got up as usual and got prepared. I picked an outfit that I'd never worn before. I had straightened my hair the night before. I had to look fly for my debut. It was a refreshing feeling when I got inside my car. The fresh new car smell is what I loved mostly. But when I arrived to my first period class it was obvious that something was wrong by the way everyone was looking at me.

As soon as I sat down at my desk my teacher called me to the front.

"Cristina I'm so sorry, but you've been terminated from the school as of today. The principal was just going to call your mom to inform her."

My mouth dropped open. I couldn't believe what I was hearing. I just knew now I couldn't go back home. I was already in enough shit with Moms. I had to think of a plan and quick. I really didn't want to be a burden on Sam but I needed him once more.

When I talked to him he agreed to put me in a hotel suite until he found me an apartment.

When I got to the suite I was amazed. I didn't even want to think of the amount he'd spent on it. I started to hang up a few of my outfits that I had managed to grab right before my mom had gotten off work. I was excited about staying here and I was even more excited because Sam had promised to take me to dinner and to spend the night. He made up some excuse to his wife, saying that his aunt had fallen ill and that she needed him to stay with her for a few nights. She'd said that she understood.

I couldn't wait because it would be our first overnight stay. I had to look perfect for my man, so I went to the salon to get my hair and nails done. Then I went and picked up some sexy lingerie then I went back to the room to get dressed. He sent a text message saying be ready for dinner around seven-thirty.

Seven-thirty sharp, Sam was outside waiting for me.

"You look amazing," he said, as he looked me up and down.

"You look nice yourself," I told him.

After dinner we headed back to the suite. "That was a good dinner," I said to him as I gave him a light peck on his cheek. I was horny and hadn't had sex in a few weeks. I wanted him so badly that just his scent alone was seducing me. I was having a few thoughts about the freaky things that I wanted to do to him tonight and I could tell he wanted me like I wanted him. His hand started playing in between my legs the whole ride back to the room. When we got inside the elevator, we couldn't stop kissing. His hands went up my dress. As soon as we made it to our room it was on. He laid me on the bed and he went up my dress and slid down my panties. I felt so relieved when he entered me. It felt like all my problems had been wiped away. I then wished it could be like this all the time but I knew that wasn't possible. When we were done I just rested my head on his chest and decided to just be grateful for the time we were able to spend with each other.

The first thing I heard when I woke up was Sam arguing on the phone. I could tell by the conversation that he was talking to his wife.

"What was that about?" I asked.

"That was my wife talking about how she called me over thirty times and I didn't respond back."

"Well, tell her you fell asleep early."

"Yeah, but then she's all like, 'then what are you staying there for if you're going to be asleep.'"

"I'm sorry," I said to him as I planted a huge kiss on his forehead.

"I knew she was calling but I was so wrapped up in what we were doing I couldn't stop. Damn, I wish it could be like this all the time."

At that moment I wanted to just blurt out, "It can happen if you would just leave her!" But I didn't want our beautiful time to get ruined with one of those arguments.

"Can I get some before I go to work?" he asked as he grabbed my ass.

"Anything you want, Daddy," I said as I pulled down his boxers and went to work. It was like we couldn't get enough of one another. After he finished letting out his load he instantly got out of the bed. It looked like he had gotten a whole lot of good sex and he couldn't get himself together.

"You coming back tonight?" I asked him in my baby voice.

"Yeah, but first I must go home and straighten out this situation. Hopefully she calms down."

He kissed my lips and headed for work. It was like I was in a dreamland. I couldn't get over my wonderful time with Sam. I got dressed and I headed over to Sharon's house.

When I arrived Sharon seemed pretty excited.

"What are you all excited about?" I asked.

"Your friend Chris just called. He said he wanted to move me down to L.A. for more video shoots."

"Oh, he did?" I asked. I must admit I was a little shocked.

"Well, he said he was trying to get a hold of you also but he couldn't reach you."

"So are you going to go?" I asked her.

"Well yeah, this is something I always wanted to do plus he said he had a room for me at his house and all. It don't seem like you're too happy for me," she said in a sad voice. "Is there something wrong with Chris?"

"Not exactly, but I think he's a Pimp."

"A Pimp, really? Not him," she said in disbelief.

"Well remember that girl I was telling you about, the one he lives with, who so-calls handles his business?"

She nodded with her eyes glued to me, waiting for me to spill the gossip.

"Well, their relationship seemed a little strange to me. One of the nights I was there he asked her to take me out. She took me to this club where it was nothing but prostitutes and pimps. All of a sudden she gets this phone call and it sounded as if she was about to turn a trick. So she told me she would be back in an hour but she took longer and when I told him he was pissed he told her to go to her room and she listened. I was amazed. That sort of changed the way I felt about him. I ain't gonna lie, I wanted to go home."

"So is that why you think he's a pimp?" she asked.

"What else could it be? Ain't no man just gonna tell no grown ass woman to go to her room and she listens. He tried to cover it up and by saying she's someone who handles business for him, but I know its way more than that."

"So you're really convinced he's a pimp?" asked Sharon once more.

"Girl yes, I know you're older but you got a lot to learn." I laughed.

"You should come, Cristina, it should be fun."

"Not right now; I'm working on my relationship with Sam. I'm so close to making him leave his wife I could feel it. He supposed to be looking for me an apartment. Anyway, you have fun and call me as soon as you get there and don't forget!"

I wasn't ready to head back to the suite just yet. Sam wasn't getting off for the next three hours and I still wasn't quite sure if he was even coming to the suite to stay with me for the night. So I stopped by the local coffee shop and ordered a hot chocolate. I sat in the corner next to a window. I sat back in my chair and I sipped my warm drink as I thought about the mess I had made for my life in the past couple of weeks. I'd managed to get myself kicked out of school. I ran away from home, and now living in a hotel. And, I'm sure my Moms called the police to report me missing. But there were also some good things: at least I had my man Sam and my spanking brand new car. My birthday was coming up in a few weeks and I would be getting my inheritance. Then I could really persuade Sam that I could be the better woman for him and hopefully he would leave his wife for good.

CHAPTER 6

A New Home

During the next few days, Sam stayed at the suite with me. He claimed the lie about taking care of his sick aunt was working. He said he was going back home the next night. I was devastated. I'd grown more attached to him. I knew I should be grateful for everything he's done for me. I didn't want to seem like I was pushing too hard but I desperately wanted Sam to tell his wife the truth: that he was in fact in love with me. The past few days I so badly wanted to bring the subject up. But I knew from past experiences he would make excuses. But hell, I didn't see why it was so hard. The truth shall set you free, as they say. All he had to do was pay her a few thousand a month and they could have joint custody of their son. I didn't see what the big deal was but, he made it seem so difficult.

I decided that I wasn't going to ruin our last night together by talking to him about leaving his wife, but in the morning I was going to bring it up whether he liked it or not.

Sam left some money for me to go to the mall to get an outfit; he also wanted me to get my hair and nails done. He told me to be ready at eight because he was going to take me to dinner. I really needed to look my best. This was my last chance for making him see things my way. I picked out a short skimpy black dress that showed off my beautiful legs and I picked out some four-inch heels.

When I got my hair done, instead of getting it flat, I had my hairdresser add a few curls. I chose French tip for my nails and feet. I was at the nail shop longer than expected and I was running late. I got to the suite as fast I could get there. I laid out my dress and my heels an all my accessories to match and I put some rollers in my hair and a scarf and a shower cap to make sure my hair wouldn't get wet.

One hour later I was looking like the flyest girl in the Bay Area.

I looked at the clock. It read eight ten. Sam was running late and that was awkward because he usually was always early and I hadn't heard from him all day. I was starting to get worried. At eight twenty I heard a knock at the door.

"Oh finally it's Sam," I said to myself excitedly. "Who is it?" I asked just to be sure.

"Room service," said a woman.

I was confused. "Ma'am I didn't order any room service." I said from the other side of the door.

"Your man wanted to surprise you with these roses and champagne; he said he would be running a little late."

How sweet of him, I thought as I opened the door. It was odd this woman wasn't wearing a uniform. I reached for the champagne and roses anyway. Next thing I knew, the woman was punching me in the face.

"What?" I was confused. She punched me again. I punched her back in the face even though I was still trying to figure out what was going on. When I punched her back that seemed to piss her off even more and that's when she busted me upside the head with the champagne bottle. I fell to the floor and she shoved the roses in my face.

Next thing I knew Sam came running in the room. "I tried to stop her but she beat me here," he cried out to me.

"Ramona, let go!" he yelled to her.

"Sick Aunt?" she yelled. "So she's the sick Aunt, huh? I was a fool for even believing in you. I knew you could never change. Fifteen years, fifteen years," she repeated, "and you still up to your no-good tricks."

I laid there on the floor with blood running down my face, still trying to suck up all the information I was hearing from Ramona. Sam grew even more heated, I guess because she was revealing the truth.

He grabbed her by her arm and he pulled her out of the suite. You could hear them arguing down the hall. I was shocked, confused and hurt. That bastard didn't even help me up or ask me if I was okay. I felt like a complete fool, especially to know I had fallen for all the lies. He claimed to have only been with her for five years. He also said he'd never before cheated on his wife with another woman; he lied about that too. She was also much prettier than he described. I wouldn't go far as to say she looked better than me, but I can say he downplayed her.

She looked as if she was around thirty-two or thirty-three. She was the color of milk chocolate, and she had long light brown hair. She had C-cup breasts and a tiny waistline. I wasn't trying to size her up like that, but I had to check out my competition.

I finally got up and went to the bathroom to see the damage to my face. It was a huge gash and it was bleeding nonstop. I grabbed a wet towel from the bathroom and I held it to my wound. She'd gotten me pretty good. Normally I would have snapped right back and whooped her ass, but I was completely taken off guard.

I didn't know what to do at this point but sit in this suite and wait to hear the news from Sam. I was hoping that he would come clean to his wife and tell her that he was in love with me, and this nightmare would be over.

Two days had gone by and I still hadn't heard a thing from Sam. A million and one thoughts ran through my head. Maybe Sam wasn't really in love with me like he claimed to be. I tried calling him a few times but it went straight to voicemail and his message box was full. I was confused about what I should do. I only had two hundred dollars left and I wasn't sure how many days he'd paid for the suite. I was depressed and, I didn't go anywhere. My hair stayed in a ponytail and I looked a mess. I barely even ate. The more time went by without me talking to him, the sicker I became.

Next thing I knew I was hearing knocks on the door. I knew the housekeepers had to see the Do Not Disturb sign on the door.

"Who is it," I yelled. Now I was really annoyed.

"It's the manager," a man replied. "Check out time was two hours ago."

I knew what that meant: Sam didn't pay for any more days. I couldn't describe the pain I was feeling. I had never felt so played in my life. I gathered all of my things as quickly as I could and I got up out of that place, not knowing what my next move would be.

I hopped in my car and just sat there for a while with my face buried inside of my steering wheel. A few tears fell as I thought about everything. I couldn't believe Sam had made such a fool out of me. I hadn't seen or heard from him since the incident, and now his phone was disconnected.

I wiped the tears from my face. I knew that now was not the time to cry, I had to plan my next move.

I then decided to go home and try to make things right with Mom.

My heart felt like it was about to jump out of my chest as I pulled up to the house. When I got to the door I took a deep breath, then I knocked. As soon as Moms saw me through the peephole she opened the door, then pulled me close to her and held me tightly as if she'd thought she had lost me forever.

"Are you okay?" she asked while she examined my face and body for bruises. "What is this on your eye, what happened to you?"

"Nothing mom, I'm alright, I'm just a little hungry." I knew she wasn't buying it. She and I both knew I looked bad; I hadn't been eating or sleeping and I had an ugly cut on my eye.

As soon as I went upstairs to my room, I noticed that my things weren't there.

"Ma, why are all of my things gone?" At this point I was totally confused.

"Well Chrissie, that's what I been meaning to talk with you about."

"What the hell is going on? Are you kicking me out now? Especially after all of the things you put me through coming up as a child?"

"See, now that's one of our big problems. I know I messed up. But you have no idea what it was like to have the only love I ever had get taken away from me just like that. And to raise two kids in that situation was hard. You don't know how hard it was for me to recover from drug addiction. My life wasn't easy and I know yours wasn't easy either coming up, but now you have it made in the shade yet you continue to take advantage of me because you know that I feel guilty for how you and Sabrina had it. I'm not going to let you hold it over my head for life. You've done gone too far now. You lied and said you were at your friend's house for the weekend but you weren't and only God knows where you were and who you were with. Now you've gotten yourself kicked out of school, you ran away and now you come home with that cut on your face. I don't know what's going on with you. So I must put my foot down once and for all. You must go and stay with your sister for the time being."

"No mom, please don't make me move in with Sabrina. Are you doing this to me because you want the master bedroom? Cause if so I will gladly trade you. Please don't make me live with her."

"Well Chrissie, in a few weeks you will be eighteen and you will inherit the rest of your money, which is three hundred thousand dollars, and then you will be able to do as you please."

"But Ma," I interrupted.

"Don't but mamma me, you were the one fussing and hollering about your money so you will be getting it very soon. For now you will be moving with your sister. Do you still want that home-cooked meal?" I could tell it was hard for her to put her foot down, but I could see that her mind was made up and she wasn't changing it.

"No, I just lost my appetite," I said as I ran out the door and slammed it behind me.

I couldn't believe this was happening. Sabrina was so nosey. I knew she would be all in my business trying to figure out how I got a phone. I knew if I was to bring my car anywhere near the house, she would find me in it and she would question me. I was frustrated but I knew I had no place else to go. Moms made it clear that it wasn't cool for me to live in her home anymore.

When I got to my sister's house I parked three blocks down. I had to be extra careful so she wouldn't be able to spot my car.

She opened the door and she greeted me with a hug. "We have a room ready for you. It's the one next to Jayden's. He requested that he be close to his auntie."

I was surprised she didn't mention any of my recent events. The good thing about staying here is that I would be able to spend quality time with my nephew. Jayden was only five but he had the mind of a fifteen year old. He always kept me laughing and smiling. I laid there across my bed feeling sad and confused. I stared at the ceiling until I fell asleep.

I was a bit irritated when my sister woke me up to tell me that she wanted to have a one-on-one talk and that she wanted to do so over breakfast. Here we go again, I thought. I decided that I would try my best to maintain a good attitude. I really wasn't interested in what she had to say, because at the end of the day it was my life and I had to live it my way.

"So what's this all about?" I asked.

"I wanted to talk to you. I'm not here to criticize you but my job

as your older sister is to make you aware of your behavior," she said
as she took a few more sips of her coffee. "You've been lying, skipping
school, sleeping with married men and only lord knows what else."

"Well big sis, you wasn't Miss perfect when you were my age
either."

"Chrissie, you ain't going to get nowhere in life with that type of
attitude. This is real. You're about to collect three hundred thousand
dollars, that's a whole lot of money. What are you going to do with
it all?"

"I plan on going to Los Angeles. I'm going to finish up high
school and then I want to enroll myself in fashion school. I will find
a part time job and then get an apartment and a car while I put the
rest of the money into some type of investment account." It wasn't
the truth but she would be satisfied with my answer.

"Well, I got to hand it to you. I'm impressed with your plans."

I was relieved. Sabrina was the last person I wanted on my back.
My real plans were to make some millions. Three hundred thousand
was a good start but I wanted more. I was going to need more if I
was going to live the life that I always wanted.

"Have you still been seeing that guy?" she asked breaking the
silence.

"No," I said with a disgusted look on my face. "Ever since you
told me he was married, I told him to get lost. Why are you asking
me that all of a sudden?"

"I heard that his wife caught him in a hotel with another woman.
He's bad news and I was just making sure that woman wasn't you."

"Not me. I don't see him anymore and I cussed him out for not
telling me he was married."

"Well good. I'm glad we had this talk because I was getting
worried about you."

We continued our breakfast as we reminisced about old times.

When we arrived back at the house Jay had already picked
Jayden up from school

"Come and give your auntie a hug."

"Where you been, Auntie?" he asked, as if he was worried about me also. I could tell mom and Sabrina had been doing some talking around him.

"Auntie's fine," I assured him as I kissed him on his forehead. He then went off to play with his toys.

We sat down at the dinner table like we were a happy family, Jayden, Jay, Sabrina and I. There was a knock at the door. It was Trey, I ran straight to the bathroom to check on my hair and my face.

"Do you want a plate Trey?" asked Sabrina.

"No, I just came to talk to your hubby real quick."

"Well there's plenty left " she said trying to convince him to have dinner with us.

"Come on, just stay." I pleaded.

"Alright, "he said as he pulled out a seat and sat down.

"So how've you been?" I asked in my sexy voice.

"Everything's been pretty good, how about yourself ?" he asked.

"Better now that you're here."

Sabrina rolled her eyes. "So let's say grace," she interrupted. "Thank you God for Bringing my beautiful family here tonight so that we can all enjoy this wonderful meal Amen," she said as she opened her eyes.

I couldn't keep my eyes off Trey. He looked so good. He must have just gotten a fresh haircut and he smelled good too. Trey was just the man I needed to make me get over my heartache with Sam.

"So how's your business going?" I asked him.

"Business is doing great, and come to speak of it; I haven't seen you at the wash house in a while."

"Well, I've been a little busy"

"Doing what?" butted in Sabrina. "It ain't like you're in school."

I gave her one of those if-looks-could-kill faces.

"So you haven't been in school?" He shook his head.

I can tell that was a complete turn off to him.

"I didn't exactly drop out. I'm going back real soon," I said, trying to make it sound better.

"Well, I hope so," added Jay.

For the rest of the evening I was pissed at Sabrina. What gave her the right to embarrass me like that in front of Trey?

I was sleeping like a baby until loud bangs at the door woke me up. "What is it?" I yelled. I was real cranky; I hadn't had any real sleep in days.

"Open the door now" Yelled Sabrina.

"Not now, Sabrina, I'm tired," I yelled back.

Next thing I knew she unlocked the door with her key.

"Cristina, Mom was right you done turned into a big liar. You still have been seeing that married man. You lied to me dead in my face. You were the woman his wife caught him cheating with."

I was half asleep but now she had fully grabbed my attention. "Where you getting all of this?" I asked her.

"My employee at the restaurant is her aunt, the same woman who spotted you two at the hotel together. I don't know what you're going to do but you have to move up out of here, you ain't my sweet baby sister anymore, You've changed, You ain't to be trusted, not in my house with my husband."

"What are you trying to say, that I will sleep with Jay? For heaven's sake, I'm your little sister! I would never do that to you."

"My little sister who runs around sleeping with married men. Yeah, that includes family too; I learned it first-hand from Nikki."

"You're comparing me to Nikki and kicking me out? Sabrina how could you?"

"And sleeping with married men, how could you?"

"Don't worry; I'm going to pack my things and I'm out of here!"

"Good," was all she said as she slammed the door.

I couldn't believe it: my own sister kicking me out. I was even more hurt by the fact that she thought I would sleep with her husband. It's not my fault I just so happened to fall in love with a married man, but I would never do such a thing to my own sister.

As I was packing my things in my suitcase I tried to figure out where to go.

I drove around in my brand new car, which was the only thing I had left. I couldn't believe that I'd been kicked out of three places within forty- eight hours. I was tired and I didn't have anywhere to go. I made a stop at the coffee shop to get some hot chocolate. As I drank my warm drink I felt a little more relaxed. I fell asleep for a half a second when I saw a repo man towing my car. I jumped up and ran outside.

"What are you doing?" I yelled. "That's my car you're towing."

"Nothing personal kid, I'm just doing my job," said the chubby Caucasian man.

"Why are you towing it?"

"It's getting repossessed."

I then knew that Sam didn't make the payment, so they had to track down the car. I knew there was nothing I could do but grab my bags. I then went back inside the coffee shop. I sat down folded my arms on the table and cried. I was not only embarrassed but I was so hurt, how could Sam put me through all of this?

As I sat at the table weeping, I felt someone tap me on my shoulder. When I turned around it was Trey.

I instantly started to wipe the tears from my eyes.

"What're you doing here?" was all I managed to get out.

"I came here to get some tea and I find you over here crying. What's the matter Lil mama?" he asked as he took a seat right next to me.

At first I was hesitant to tell him what was going on but then it all just came right out. "Trey, I really don't have any place to go. Mom and Sabrina kicked me out."

He grabbed a tissue from the table and handed it to me.

"You mean to tell me both your sister and your mom kicked you out?"

"It's a long, long story and I really don't want to talk about it right now," I said as I went in for the kill and leaned on his shoulder. I sobbed even louder, and I knew that made him slightly uncomfortable but he eventually put his arms around me to hug me back. I was enjoying every second because it was the nicest he's ever been to me. "Can I stay with you until I can get things settled with my moving situation?" I asked him.

"You know your mom and sister ain't gonna let you be homeless. I bet whatever it is all you have to do is say sorry and they will let you back in but I bet it's your pride getting in the way."

He did have a point: mom would let me back in if she knew that I absolutely had nowhere else to go and so would Sabrina. All I had to do was just admit I was wrong. But my pride wouldn't let that happen. Hell, they'd done things to me that they needed to be apologizing about. Moms for being on drugs and leaving me in the system, and Sabrina for leaving me also. One way or the other I wasn't kissing their Asses.

I cried even louder and I knew that I would be able to convince him.

"Okay, but only for a few days. Just until you get it together to where you can apologize to your mom."

"OK," I said as I wiped the tears from my face.

CHAPTER 7

Living with Trey

When I woke up, I still couldn't believe I was sleeping at Trey Steven's house. Things were looking better already and a plan was forming in my head. As soon as I got my money I wanted propose a few business plans to Trey. If he was a real man he would recognize a real woman. I was good looking, I had a great body, I was smart, I knew how to dress, I knew how to present myself well and I was going to be paid. He would be crazy to pass all of that up.

Trey's two-bedroom apartment was very clean, cold and modern—something that described him. He was clean-cut and edgy, but at the same time he could be cold, especially if he wasn't too fond of you.

The guest bedroom was clean and relaxing, something I could deal with until he moved me into his room. He made it clear that I was to make myself at home. He promised that he would cook me dinner so that I could feel better and I was looking forward to it. It was going to be like a date. Even though deep down inside I knew that he didn't view it as a date, just the thought of the two of us being alone having dinner in his home was like a date to me.

I added some sexy loose curls to my jet-black long hair. I looked inside my suitcase and found one of my favorite designer dresses. It was short and black with a lace trim. I put on my 24-karat gold hoop earrings and my 24- karat bangles and my 24-karat necklace with my name engraved on it. My finishing touch was my lip-gloss. I looked in the mirror one last time and I knew I looked super hot.

When Trey came home he had a woman with him. I was a little surprised but when I looked at the woman she looked older and she resembled him so I figured she was his mom.

"Cristina, this is my mom, Mrs. Stevens, Mom, this is Cristina."

"Pleased to meet you," I told her, even though I wasn't expecting this at all. Otherwise I would have worn something much more appropriate, and I was disappointed by the fact that I wasn't going to be spending alone time with Trey like I expected.

Trey pulled me aside. "Do you mind putting some pants or tights under that shirt you call a dress? Mom's a little old fashioned and all. I'm sure you understand

I was a little embarrassed but I went in the room and put on some tights, knowing that's what I should have worn in the first place.

"Much better," said Mrs. Stevens as I came back out of the room. I wanted to tell her to mind her business but I couldn't, say that to my future mother in law so I bit my tongue. I could tell he was her only child by the way she treated him. She went behind him cleaning up as he cooked. She critiqued his cooking and I could tell he was annoyed a bit but he loved her and he didn't have the heart to tell her to leave him alone, so he told her to go in the living room to keep me company. She wasn't too thrilled about it but she joined me in the living room anyway.

"So young lady, how old are you?" she asked.

"I'm seventeen but I will be turning eighteen in a couple of weeks."

"So what brings you here with my son?"

"It's kind of a long story, My mom and I aren't getting along to well, so Trey was letting my stay over here a few days until things cool down."

"So where do you know him from?"

"He's my brother in law Jays best friend."

"So Sabrina Brown is your sister?"

"Yes"

"Oh, I like her, she's a real good girl, Jay got lucky with her, I sure hope Trey finds him a girl like that."

I instantly became annoyed; everyone always favored Sabrina, Miss goodie two shoes.

"So are you planning on going to college?"

"Yeah, sure," I responded.

"Yeah, sure," she repeated after me, in other words saying yeah, right you ain't going to no college.

"Well you're a pretty young lady and I hope you go to college. And I hope you will find a good man, maybe like a southern guy, and stay away from those hoodlums in the streets." I knew she was basically trying to say find a good man other than her son but if only she knew he was my target and I always get what I want. It was my way or the highway, usually, but Trey was making things a lot tougher than I had anticipated. Still, I was sure that I was going to get him to eventually come around.

"Dinner's ready," said Trey. I was more than excited to eat and I was more than ready to end the conversation with Mrs. Stevens.

His mom did teach him well in the kitchen, because dinner was amazing and I could go for him cooking for me all the time; he looked real good preparing dinner. He didn't look gay or anything like that; it was just that he was sexy with just about anything he did in my eyes. At first Mrs. Stevens wasn't too fond of me but as the night went on I could tell she warmed up.

When it was time for her to leave she gave me a hug. I felt

satisfied knowing that my possible mother-in-law took a small liking to me.

Over the next couple of days I did everything in my power to get Trey to consider the possibility of me being his woman. I cleaned his whole house from top to bottom. Not saying that it wasn't already clean, but while I was here I wasn't letting this chance to stay with the man of my dreams go to waste.

I could tell he wasn't getting any pussy because he was so damn uptight all the time. I just wanted to jump butt naked in his bed and rock his world so good he could never think about another woman. I had a big vision for us. As soon as I collected my inheritance, I wanted to propose a couple of ideas to him. I knew he had what it took to make things happen, since he already owned his own carwash and the café that was inside the carwash. I was sure he could a chick like me on his side.

The night before my birthday, I wanted to cook Trey a special dinner. I was going to cook him his favorite, pasta. I wasn't the cooking type, but for Trey it was worth a try. I looked online for a recipe and then I went to the store and bought all the ingredients. I followed the instructions step by step. I came out with a beautiful dish. I took a shower, applied some makeup, sprayed perfume, and I was ready to see my baby.

He got in around ten looking like he'd had a rough day.

"What's that smell?" he asked as he sniffed his way to the kitchen.

"I cooked you a pasta dish since I know you love pasta."

"I'm impressed," he said. He went to put up his things and he washed his hands then he went to grab a plate.

"No, no, I got it baby, go have a seat, I will make it for you. I know you just got off work and you're tired. Besides I wanted to show my appreciation for you letting me stay here and all."

"Okay," he said as he smiled. He sat on the couch and turned on the basketball game.

"Dinner was great Cristina. I must admit I didn't take you for the cooking type and I'm especially impressed since you did all of this and you're the one having a birthday in less than an hour."

"Well there are a lot of things I would do for you if you were my man. You deserve it."

"I appreciate you saying that, lil mama."

"Do you mind if I sat here next to you and watch the game?"

"Have a seat," he said.

I didn't really want to watch the game. I didn't care about sports. I just wanted to sit and watch him. I could sit and watch him all day. The way his face looked while he was concentrating on watching the game was sexy. The way he drank his beer was even sexy.

I looked at the time; it was midnight: my birthday.

"I know I'm not twenty-one yet and I know you don't condone underage drinking and all, but can we at least have some shots for my birthday?"

"Alright I guess we can do one shot for your birthday, I can't believe I'm pouring you a shot, lil mama. But it's all good; you're safe here with me." "Cheers to new beginnings," I said, and then we took our shots.

I was so happy my birthday was starting out right. I don't know what came over me and where I got my courage. But I started to massage his back. To my surprise he didn't stop me, he just mumbled, "Ummmm, this feels good." I got closer and I started massaging him more intensively. I noticed his eyes started to roll in the back of his head. I knew it was hard to resist, especially since he hadn't had a woman's touch in a while. I decided to test my luck and go a bit further with it. I moved my hands from over the top of his shirt to under his shirt. He still didn't stop me. That's when I decided to go in for the kill. I started to tongue kiss his neck and still he didn't stop me; instead he started to kiss me back. I couldn't believe we were making out. His kisses were so sweet and tender. His hands went up my shirt and he grabbed my breasts firmly. I felt my panties getting soaked he then surprised me and jumped on top of me. By now I felt his hard penis poking at me. Then he stopped. I felt like my whole world had ended.

"Let's go in my bedroom," he said as he reached for my hands. I followed. He then reached for a condom out of the drawer. He took off his pants. I instantly took off my clothes; I wasn't going to make things difficult. I knew I wanted this more than anything. He started out kissing my inner thighs and he slowly worked his way toward my dripping wet pussy. I just knew I would wake up at any moment. He was licking and sucking and putting his finger in all at the same time; I came within minutes. Then he entered me from behind and he made me come once again; this time we came together. When we were done there was a strange silence for minutes.

"That was just what I needed. I didn't know you had it like that," I was so happy that I had just released my sexual tension that was built up in me. The room was silent. I must say I was disappointed at the weird awkwardness. Trey seemed to be thinking and thinking real hard. "What's the matter baby? You didn't enjoy it or something?" I asked.

"Of course I did, but now I wonder did I just make a huge mistake."

"A mistake about what? I'm eighteen now if that's what you're worried about."

"I got some thinking to do," he said. He got out of the bed and he put on his clothes and he left. I was greatly disappointed but I just got up put on my clothes and I went back in the guest room. One hour later I heard him coming in the house. Now I was confused. I really didn't know what to think now. All that night I didn't get much sleep.

The day that I had been waiting for had arrived. It was my birthday and I made it clear to Trey that I didn't want to spend it with anyone but him. I also told him that I had something very important that I wanted to discuss with him. He also made it clear that he wanted to discuss something with me also. I wondered what he wanted to talk with me about. I was hoping he was feeling the same way I was feeling.

I called my mom earlier and the plan was still set for me to get my money. I didn't waste any time. I was down to my last fifty dollars and I hadn't been this broke in years.

I got dressed and I made my way over to my mom's. When she saw me she wasn't excited like she would have normally been. She looked as if she was giving me a curse instead of three hundred thousand dollars.

"Now Chrissie, I know this isn't going to make you rich but this here is a lot of money for an eighteen-year-old. I highly suggest you get yourself back into school and graduate. I want you to be careful how you spend this money. Watch the company you keep and pay attention to your surroundings." I knew what she was telling me was right. But I wasn't really trying to hear all that, because if she and Sabrina loved and cared for me so much they would have never kicked me to the curb. I was trying to get out of this lecture as soon as possible and get down to collecting my cash.

After the transaction was completed, I felt like a brand new person. The next move I was going to make was to the car lot to buy my birthday present. I was going to buy my third Mercedes Benz in one year. This time I wanted a Clk 550, all white pearl coat. It would end up costing ninety thousand, which left me with two hundred and ten thousand dollars. I knew for the average person I was doing a bit much. But hey, I'd been having a Mercedes since I was first able to drive and that was the way that I was going to continue things.

As I drove off the lot I felt like a million dollars. My next stop was to the mall. I bought a Dolce and Gabbana dress and a Fendi bag. I bought a couple pairs of jeans, two pairs of stilettos and one pair of boots. I even picked my baby up some cologne and I also picked him out a fly leather jacket. My next stop was to the salon. I had to get my hair, nails, and feet done. It's been a while since I had visited any salon and by now it was much needed. A couple of hours later I was looking beautiful and I was now ready to go to dinner with my man.

When he saw me he looked amazed. "Wow, you look beautiful," he said as he handed me some flowers. When he saw my car his mouth fell open.

"You like?" I asked him.

"It's beautiful, but how could you ever afford something like this? You don't even have a place to live." He shook his head as if I was wrong for treating myself to a present that I well deserved.

"Well I'm ready to go when you are," he said.

As soon as we were seated we ordered our food I was ready to start talking, but Trey started first.

"There's something that I've wanted to talk with you about. I don't want you to get offended and take what I'm saying in a wrong way. It's just that you've been living here at my house for a few weeks now. I originally told you a few days. I didn't want to press the issue because I know that you have been stressed out. You were getting moved from one home to the next. But now I see that you've come across some money, You've bought yourself not just and ordinary but a top of the line vehicle, I wanted to know when were you planning on moving?"

"Is that the important news you had to tell me?" I was now disappointed.

"Well yeah, I'm not kicking you out on the streets or anything. I had a talk with your mother and she said she would be more than happy to have you come back home if you've learned your lesson."

"You went and talked to my mom without me, how dare you?"

"Look, I've done my part in helping you. I don't owe you anything. I didn't mean to confuse you last night. You were walking around half-dressed and I let my wants and desires knock me off track. You knew what you were doing, Cristina."

I felt my heart break in half. All the dreams that I had planned for us suddenly went out the door.

"You wait all the way until my birthday to break this news to me?"

"Lil mama, I originally told you a few days and it's been well over that. Now I figure since you got some money in your pocket, you will be fine."

"But Trey, I'm in love with you. I have so many plans for us."

"Look sweetheart, you're young and beautiful. You have your whole life ahead of you. You need to be trying to focus on finishing school and maybe college. Maybe you will join a sorority or something, who knows, anything but playing house-wife with me."

"I get your concerns, but I know what I want. I want you I've been wanting you since I was thirteen."

He paused for a moment and he put his head down "I didn't want to just come out and tell you but I'm actually seeing someone and she's coming into town in a few days."

I couldn't describe the pain that I was feeling when he broke that one down to me. One by one everyone I knew was letting me down.

"So what did you want to talk to me about?"

"Never mind, it doesn't even matter now that you got a woman and you're kicking me out. Thanks for breaking the news to me on my eighteenth birthday." The tears were pouring down my face uncontrollably. "Let's go now; I officially just lost my appetite."

When we got back to the house, I immediately started packing my things.

"Lil mama, I wasn't talking about leaving tonight. I didn't mean to ruin your birthday, I promise."

"You didn't just ruin my birthday, you ruined my life," I said as I kept throwing things into my suitcase.

"I'm good enough to sleep with but I'm not good enough to be your woman huh? You're cold-blooded, Trey." I was on my way towards exiting the house.

He then placed his strong arms onto my shoulders and he squeezed me tightly. "You going to be alright, lil mama, I know you will."

I didn't hug him back. I didn't say anything. I just walked out the door.

Trey thought I was going to my mamma's house, but he was wrong. I was going to L.A. Since I had nobody on my team in my hometown, I decided to move on and start all over. I had just turned eighteen. I was now free to do what I wanted and with who I wanted and when I wanted. Nobody could tell me anything. I was going to prove everyone wrong. I was going to prove to my sister and mom that I was the smarter one. I was going to make Trey wish he had chosen me instead of whomever. I had two hundred thousand plus in my bank account and I was ready to shake some things up in So-Cal.

CHAPTER 8

Moving to So-Cal

Five-and-a-half hours later I had arrived in L.A. The air was different. Everyone seemed to have banging bodies. Most of the women had fake breasts and fake hair and some type of plastic surgery. This city was fast and fun and I couldn't wait to dive head first into it.

I made a stop to the Nextel store and I copped me a new phone. I reached in my purse for the sheet of paper where I had numbers written down. I dialed up Sharon.

"Hey Cristina, haven't heard form you in a while, how you been? So much has happened. There's so much I got to tell you girl that I don't know where to begin. But enough about me, what's been going on with you? How are you and your man doing?"

She was running her mouth like ninety miles per hour. I could see a big difference in her already.

"Guess what? I'm in L.A."

"What?" she yelled. "Hell no, I don't believe you. Where's Sam?"

"Things didn't quite work with Sam and I. But hey, I'm not crying or complaining. I'm here in this new city and I'm excited."

"Where you staying?" she asked me.

"I don't know, I was thinking that maybe I can stay at Chris's house if he is still cool with that."

"Girl, I'm sure he is more than cool with that. Girl, we going to have so much fun," she said excitedly.

She didn't seem like her normal quiet self. She actually seemed happy. It was a little strange that she was living with a guy that I had been dating, even though I was only dating him for a real short period of time. I was almost sure he was a pimp, and I also knew Sharon was a bit naive and she wasn't up on the street game. I'm sure Chris was feeding her plenty of bullshit. I just hoped she was smart enough to stay focused on her goals, which were modeling and acting.

When I arrived at his home, Sharon greeted me with a hug. "I missed you, girl. I can't begin to explain how happy I am that you came here."

As Chris made his way down the stairs my heart started to beat faster. I didn't know how Chris felt about me not returning his phone calls.

"Hey stranger?" said Chris as he greeted me with a hug. "You just disappeared on a brother huh?"

"No, not really I had a few issues going on at the house that's all."

"Well is it money problems, because I told you I can help you with that."

"You can first start by helping me take these bags in the house."

"You ain't changed a bit," he said as he laughed and grabbed my two biggest bags.

Later that evening, Sharon and I took a drive on the Sunset Strip. We had a lot to catch up on. These people in southern Cali were different; everyone seemed to be busy and at the same time enjoying life. When we arrived at the diner we ordered salads and iced teas. Food that went well with the summer, plus we were trying to keep our figures on point.

"So girl what finally brings you down here? It's about time."

"Well Sam and I didn't work out because One day I just woke up and realized he was too old for me. A girl like me really couldn't stand the thought of breaking up his family. I was mainly thinking about the child, so I told him it would be best if we went our separate ways." I couldn't tell her the truth about how badly Sam had humiliated me when his wife caught us together; how he'd cut off all ties with me and left me out in the cold.

"Wow, I'm just really shocked because before I left you were so excited that you guys were finally going to be together."

"Yeah that is what I thought until I got my inheritance and I thought clearly about everything and realized that I am young, beautiful and sexy, and I have money in my pockets. I realized there was more to see in life, so I thought it would be a great idea to come and chill with you guys and so far I'm loving this place. So what you been up to you little slut?" I said, teasing her. "You ain't the same Sharon I knew. You done got out here and turned into a woman."

We both laughed.

"Well, I've been in three music videos and in two magazines. I love the experience and the exposure but there ain't really any money in that. So I have been doing a little light service work with Chris."

"Service work? You mean escort service, prostitution. Don't try to make it sound good."

"Well, we call it service work and I don't have sex with these guys or Chris if that's what you're thinking."

"You ain't got to explain nothing to me, that's your business. I'm not judging, and I'm no hater. Get your money," I told her.

"Girl, all you have to do is go on a date, massage their egos. A little touching and feeling is involved but not anything that I can't handle. All the guy really wants is some attention and reassurance."

"Oh really, I said. I thought Sharon was hilarious thinking she was gaming me about something. I wanted to tell her to not let the game eat her alive.

"So are you cool with Veronica?" I asked her.

"Yeah she's pretty cool just as long as I don't get to close to Chris. He is a mess. I could hear him coming out of Veronica's room in the morning and on some nights he's even tried coming in mine. I didn't let him. I didn't know what he had going on with you."

"Oh girl it was nothing. We never had sex. We did a light drunk make out session a couple of times but nothing serious so if you want him go for it."

I didn't really mean it of course, I didn't want my friend going out with someone that I've dated but I just was testing her to see where her head was.

Later on that night, Chris wanted to take us out and I was down. I was here to have a good time. We rode in a stretch limo. Chris was the big show in town; he had to outdo every one. But that was fine by me. I liked to live large especially when this was free to me.

When we pulled up in front of the club all eyes were glued on us. Chris had three fine women rolling with him. When we went in we all headed to our VIP section where there was a bottle of platinum Patron awaiting us.

"Let's make a toast," called out Chris. "Let's toast to a baller like me and to beautiful women like you ladies and to everyone getting money." We put our shots up in the air and we drank them down. By now I was feeling good and ready to mingle.

Veronica sat next to Chris. She kept her arms around him tightly. She wasn't letting up. She felt like she had to work harder because there was now another beautiful woman in the house. Sharon and I walked around the club taking a peek at the men. To my surprise Sharon knew some of them. It was a bit odd because the Sharon I knew wasn't a social bug.

"So which ones got the money?" I asked as I was scouting out a few cutie pies.

"Mostly all of them, this is a high rollers club."

Two men approached us. I checked them out from head to toe.

They were both wearing Armani suits and one was slimmer and taller and one was a little heavier.

"So what's your name?" asked the tall slender one.

"I'm Cristina and this is my girl Sharon."

"This is my boy Marcus and I am Kevin. Can we buy you ladies some drinks?"

"Sure," I said. I was always down for a free drink.

"So do you ladies live out here?"

"Sharon moved out here like a month ago and this is actually my first night out here, so I will be looking for a place soon."

"So you guys are considered fresh meat."

"Yep," we both said in unison.

"So what do you ladies do for a living?"

"I'm about to go to school."

"Oh what college are you going to?" he asked.

"I'm going to UCLA." I was lying through my teeth knowing that I didn't even complete high school.

"I work for a service," Sharon said very proudly.

Marcus gave her a smile like he knew exactly what she had meant.

"Can we step aside Miss Sharon? I wanted to talk to you a little about that service," said Marcus.

Twenty minutes later Sharon was leaving with Marcus. Chris, Veronica and I left the club an hour before they shut down.

When we got back to Chris's home Veronica was trying to be all over him, but he wasn't feeling her, at least not at the moment. I could tell he was excited to see me. All three of us sat on the couch. Veronica put her arms around him but he instantly moved her hand and he got up out his seat and he poured two glasses of champagne. He handed one to me and he kept one for himself. I guess he was hinting to Veronica that she wasn't wanted in this conversation. She got really mad and jumped up out of her seat and pranced into her room. I laughed, I thought it was funny and I didn't care one way or the other; I didn't like the bitch no way.

He instantly turned all of his attention to me.

"I missed you Cristina," he said in a low, sexy voice. "And you never were gonna call a nigga huh? You a cold piece of work!"

"Don't sound like that. I did like you but I just had a few things going on with school and homework and living with Moms and being under eighteen and all."

"Who do you think you're fooling? You ain't a girl that's into school and I am not trying say that you dumb because I know that you sharp as hell. It's just that school aint your thing, I can tell."

"So what do you think is my thing?" I asked.

You more into the Hollywood style of life, looking glamorous, spending time getting your hair and nails done and doing yoga, getting facials shopping you know those types of things. I got a proposition for you. I know Sharon and Veronica ain't as smart as you to pull this off."

"If it's got anything to do with your services in all I want no part in it."

"Of course not. I wouldn't even approach you like that. I know you better than that."

"What do you have in mind?" I asked him.

"You know I got a few hustles going on, right? I got mad hookup on a cocaine line. I will need for you to move some of it for me to other states. This job isn't just for anyone. I believe that you're smart enough to pull it off. It's a lot of money involved too."

"Well let me ask you this: how come you don't move all your shit yourself? That way you can keep all your money." I was skeptical with these types of things because people usually don't let you in on their money.

"Because baby, you a girl. The police ain't gonna sweat you and the police been kind of watching a brother for some other shit I got going on and besides I'm trying to hook you up, put some money in your pockets while you out here and eventually I want to make you my girl."

I heard what he was saying; I heard the money part, that is.

"So how much are we talking and what all I got to do?" I asked.

"I will need you to move five hundred thousand dollars worth of shit and you get ten percent. The first run is New York. You think you can hang?"

''Another fifty thousand sounded good to add to my account.

"Alright, count me in."

"Alright, I will book you a flight for next week."

CHAPTER 9

Pushing Dope

*I*t was time for me to make my first run. I was headed to New York City. I was nervous and excited all at the same time. This was my first trip to New York but I was only going to be staying for the night then I was to return back to L.A.

It took a little longer than I expected to tape the drugs on me. I was getting hot and irritated, especially with Chris. He kept running down the same rules to me over and over. He was now beginning to make me nervous.

When I got to the security checkpoint my heart was beating at a thousand miles per minute. My body started to shake and I felt sweat dripping down the side of my face.

Stay cool, stay calm, I kept on reminding myself. We had to take off our shoes, belts, earrings hair clips and all. It felt like we were stripping right there in the airport. I made sure I took off everything that was metal. I wasn't going to be going back in forth through that metal detector. I passed through the first time and I was relieved.

When I got on the plane I felt much better. I tried to make

myself as comfortable as I possibly could with the dope taped on me. I knew I had a long ride ahead of me.

When I stepped off the plane I felt the warm air of New York, I smelled all the different food in the air, the pizza and the hotdogs. The lights were bright, the buildings were tall, the air was warm and there were people everywhere and all in a hurry. I was a bit disappointed that this was strictly a business trip and I was to return very early the next day. I finally made it outside to the cars and a woman in a black BMW spotted me. She unlocked the door and I got inside.

We finally arrived in a tall building. I removed all the dope that I had on my body. She handed me two cases full of hundred dollar bills. She examined the dope. She took a little on her finger and she tasted it. She gave me the thumbs up meaning that she was pleased with the product. She then drove me to the hotel room Chris had arranged for me to stay in.

"That easy" I said to myself. "That's all it take a quick exchange and bam you get rewarded a lump sum of cash. I can definitely get use to this," I said as I ran my self a warm bath, I got out the tub, rubbed lotion all over my body and threw on something comfy and ordered me some room service while I kicked back until I fell asleep.

When I made it back to Cali, Chris was proud of me.

"See, I knew you could pull it off," he chanted. "My plan worked out like a charm. If we do this a few more times we'll be rich, just you and me baby," he said as he kissed my hand.

I didn't know exactly what his plans were but I had plans of my own and they didn't include him. I was just going to act like I was his right-hand man and make a few more moves like this until I become a millionaire.

He gave me my cut of fifty thousand that was cool, but he was making all the money. I knew that I couldn't make as much as him especially when I put in no investment. I instantly knew what I had to do. I had to invest the fifty thousand right back.

Veronica and Sharon were really getting along and I was getting a bit jealous. Sharon was supposed to be my friend; she wasn't supposed to be getting along with my enemy. I wasn't going to let her see that things were getting to me, I was way to proud for that.

Sharon asked me to go to the salon with her to get a facial and our hair and nails done. We sat in the spa chairs while they served us champagne and strawberries.

"So what's been going on Chrissie? I know we're in the same house but it's like I don't get to hang out with you much."

"Haven't been up to too much," I told her.

"So, I'm curious, what did Chris send you out to New York for?" she asked.

"He didn't tell you?"

"No, he acts like it's some secret."

I guess Chris did not want Veronica or Sharon in his business otherwise he would have told them.

"He sent me to look for us an apartment out there." I made up that lie fast.

"That little devil, always trying to surprise me," she said as she smiled to herself. "Are you sure you and Chris don't have anything going on?"

"Are you starting to catch feelings for him or something?" I asked.

"Somewhat, but it's just weird because Veronica's always going to be in the way. She's cool and everything but I just don't see how I could really be with him if she's always going to be around. She hates you because she sees you as a threat and she would hate me if she knew I was starting to like him.

"Yeah that does sound weird," I told her.

Please don't say anything, Chrissie, he asked me to join him and Veronica in a threesome."

"What, are you serious?" I laughed. "So what did you say?"

"I just laughed it off. I couldn't tell if he was serious or not, then he changed the subject. So do you think he's serious?"

"He's a man, yes he's serious," I told her as I laughed. I couldn't believe how naive she was.

Chris thought he was the man. He thought he was playing all of us. But I was playing him. I didn't have a love interest in him. Not to say he wasn't good looking, because he was. He was just the kind of man that wanted his cake and to eat it too. I could tell that he was used to playing women and he could get just about anything he wanted from them. I wasn't having it, especially when I think about all the hell Sam put me through. He could run his game or think he was running his game, but I was about to run a game of my own. I wanted to invest my money in the cocaine. That way I could pull in a few more dollars a little faster. I could get mine and get out and then work on my new life which included getting a new home on the beach which had been a dream of mine every since I was a little girl.

When I first approached him about my idea he seemed uncertain.

"What, that fifty thousand wasn't enough for you? You know that's way more than what Sharon and Veronica make put together in a month."

"Look, I'm not trying to be ungrateful," I assured him. "I just thought I'd ask. I mean why not try to invest? In the long run it works out for both us. The more money we invest together the more we can buy." By now he was thinking about what I was saying and how it made sense.

"You know Boo, that's what I like about you. Always thinking outside of the box. And what you're saying is making sense. The more money we invest the more we can make."

I grew excited knowing that I would be seeing big dollars.

"So tomorrow next stop will be Miami. You're going to have twice that shit taped on you. Do you think you can handle it?"

"Yeah of course; it's worth it."

The next day I flew out to Miami. I made the same simple transaction. When I made it home I was two hundred thousand dollars richer. This was the perfect job for me. No long hours and no labor and lots of money.

When I got home I noticed that Sharon was sort of acting funny with me. I walked in on her and Veronica giggling on the couch.

"What's so funny?" I interrupted.

"Oh nothing," they both said in unison. They both got quiet. I automatically assumed they were talking about me. It was clear they had some jealousy issues going on. But it was all good: Sharon could be friends with that little bitch because I had bigger and better plans. While they were all goggle-eyed for Chris, I was playing him and getting a bigger piece of the pie than both of them put together, and I didn't intend on having them in my business either.

My biggest move was yet to come. Chris wanted me to drive three million dollars worth of cocaine to Houston. He said this time I wasn't going to be able to tape that much cocaine on me. He made it clear that this would be my hardest move yet. He tried to make me nervous but I wasn't. I had a valid driver's license, no criminal record, and no felonies. It was all good. He made sure the dope was hidden perfectly in case any police were to pull us over.

He was sending his buddy Travis on the trip with me. He claimed that I would need help with the drive but the truth was he wanted Travis to baby-sit me and make sure I didn't run off with the three million dollars.

We were eight hours into the trip when we got pulled over by the police. This wasn't good, especially when Travis was lighting up blunt after blunt. I knew the car smelled like it was filled with marijuana. I hurried up and rolled down the windows and sprayed some perfume spray that I had in my purse. I pulled over on the side of the dark road and I was scared to death because we were somewhere in the desert and I had no clue where.

At this very moment I wish I wouldn't have gotten myself into this mess; now I could be facing the rest of my life behind bars. My heart was pumping as if it was about to fall out of my chest.

The two cops were both white men in their late forties.

"Ma'am we pulled you over because the speed limit is sixty miles per hour and you were going seventy-five." Said the officer in his southern Texas accent.

"I'm so sorry officer; I didn't notice"

"The car smells like marijuana, have you been smoking pot and driving?" he asked me.

I sobered up real quick. "No sir, I haven't. We just dropped off my older sister and she was smoking the pot, sir." The officer looked as if he didn't believe a word I was saying. He flashed his flashlight directly into my eyes.

"Well do you guys mind if I check the car out a little?" asked the other officer. My first thought was to tell him hell no, because he didn't have a search warrant.I paused for a short second.

"Sure go ahead," I told him. I was cooperating with them all the way; I didn't want them suspecting me of anything else.

The officer took a look around and he checked in the back and in the front but didn't find anything.

"You guys are free to go."

I let out a huge sigh of relief, that was way to close. I warned Travis no more smoking pot on the road; I was not trying to get caught up with millions of dollars in cocaine on me. I was nervous on the rest of trip but we made it to Houston and I didn't know if I wanted to continue on pushing drugs. Hell, I didn't need to anymore; I was going to be set, once we were done with this move.

When we made it back home, Chris felt like he was on top of the world. His net worth was now over twenty million. He bought a Bentley, a Maserati, and a Porsche. He also bought Veronica and Sharon brand new cars. Veronica picked out a red Lexus. Sharon picked out the same exact car as mine except hers was silver.

I wasn't surprised: Sharon wasn't really her own person. She was influenced by everyone around her.

Chris wanted all of us to go out together. He wanted to celebrate his new fortune.

He wanted to go all out by getting a stretched hummer limo and bottle service. We were rolling like big timers.

When we were all seated in the VIP section drinking Grey Goose and cranberry juice, Chris made his way over to me and he sat down.

"So have you been considering you and me getting together?"

"Yeah, I've been giving it some thought."

"So, like when do you think you will know? I've been asking you the same shit for the past couple of weeks now. How much more time do you think you will need?"

I could tell he was getting upset.

He put another pill in his mouth and drank it down with the Grey Goose and cranberry. He then pulled out some more pills and he started passing them around like they were candy.

"What are these?" I asked Sharon while I still held the pill in my hand.

"It's called an E pill" she said as she put her pill in her mouth and swallowed it like a pro.

"E- pill?" I said, still looking confused.

"Ecstasy pills," she said as if I was stupid.

"I think I'm going to pass this time; you can have mine."

"Sure, I will save it for later," she said as she put the pill inside of her purse.

I didn't know what that pill had inside of it so I wasn't taking it.

Chris was more than upset with me. He was pressuring me to be his girl but I don't know who in the hell he thought he was: he had two more girls living with him and I guess I was just supposed to ignore that part and be with him. The reason why I dealt with him was because he had plenty of friends, money and connections and now I was a millionaire for being under his wing.

Later on that night when we got home Chris, Sharon and Veronica were drunk and high. Chris took at least three pills and Veronica and Sharon had about two each. They were so high they were being a bit touchier feely then normal and they were laughing at some of the dumbest things. I definitely wasn't in the mood for any of that nonsense and besides I had to get up early. I had an appointment to look at a home.

I woke up out of my sleep at four o clock in the morning. I heard some loud noises. I quickly jumped out of bed. I looked around the house. I noticed that the lights were still on in the family room. I cut them off. I then heard more noises and they were growing louder but I couldn't quite make them out and it was close to Sharon's room. I decided to go in to check on her to see if she was all right. I knocked once then I opened the door. I couldn't believe what I was seeing: Veronica had her head buried in between Sharon's legs while Chris was naked sitting in the chair watching, with a patron bottle in his hand Sharon seemed to be enjoying it all until she saw me. She instantly pushed Veronica's head away and she closed her legs.

"Don't let me ruin the party" I said, as I walked away. Chris was getting his fantasy after all.

The next day was a bit awkward. Sharon, Chris and Veronica could barely look me in my eyes. I really wasn't surprised by what I saw. You couldn't expect much from two prostitutes and a pimp.

After taking a look at homes, I saw one that sparked my interest. I would be leasing the home for a year and since I had cash money I got my keys that same day.

My three-bedroom, three-story home was to die for. The main room had marble floors a chandelier hanging from the high ceilings. The kitchen had tons of cabinet space, marble countertops, a dishwasher and a small island in the middle.

My bedroom had a closet in it the size of a small bedroom. I had a balcony outside of my bedroom window. I also had a Jacuzzi and a swimming pool. I couldn't find a house on the beach. But none of that mattered now. I had falling in love with my new home. I was proud of myself. I was only eighteen years old and I manage to get a home that most people would die for.

I dreaded going back to Chris's house for my things and breaking the news to him but I knew it had to be done.

When I got to the house only Sharon and Veronica was home. Sharon half said hello and Veronica didn't say anything. I went into the room in which I was staying and packed up the few things I had and I placed them inside my car. I guess Sharon could tell I was moving and Veronica couldn't wipe that smile off her face.

When I went back for my last bag Sharon stopped me. "Can I talk to you for a second?"

"Yes, what's up?"

"I didn't know you were moving."

"Yeah it was a spur-of-the-moment kind of thing."

"Does Chris know?" she asked me.

"No, I haven't talked to him. I was going to tell him but he's not here so can you tell him for me?"

"Sure, no problem, but are you moving out because of the other night?"

"No, no don't be silly Sharon."

"It's just I was drunk and high off that ecstasy. We had been smoking a lot of weed and I don't know, it seemed like everything was happening so fast and the next thing I knew I was having a threesome."

"Well Sharon it's not up to me to judge you. You can do what you want with your life but I do have some advice: "Watch them two people you living with, and one more thing lay off those pills."

"I hope you come and visit sometimes you know I'm going to miss you around here," she said as she hugged me.

"I will," I told her. I was bittersweet about everything but it was time to move on.

No more than two hours later I received a phone call from Chris.

"So Cristina, you were just going to up and leave like that without telling me? Are you mad at me for the other night?"

"No Chris, it was just time for me to move on. I was going to have to find my own place eventually. A good deal came around and I couldn't pass it up."

"As much as I would like for you to stay with me I guess I understand. I still need your help in helping me move my shit around; you the best one for the job and I can't see Sharon executing something like that and I don't trust Veronica all the way sometimes."

"I really don't want to be involved with that activity anymore that last run in Texas scared the shit out of me, and I honestly thought I was gong jail."

"How you gonna pay your rent for that house you just moved into? How you going to keep up your lifestyle? You aint got that much money to be talking about throwing in the towel, and living out here in sunny Southern California costs and you're a high maintenance chick, So I know that money ain't gone last forever and I can't picture you getting no regular job. So what do you say? This time we get to go to Miami and I'm coming with you. We can take a mini-vacation out there too, so what do you say?"

"How much money is involved with this one?"

"Like three million and how about I give you half a million? You really can't beat that Cristina, people would die for these opportunities and yet I'm hooking you up."

I thought about it and I couldn't pass up a half a million dollars and a trip but I knew that I was playing with fire.

"Okay."

"Perfect, be ready tomorrow morning. Meet me at my house at eight o'clock sharp."

I was nervous to go on a trip with just Chris. I knew that by Sharon and Veronica not being there he was going to push himself on me or he was going to start talking that relationship crap and I wasn't interested. He was a pimp who was in denial about being one, he had too many women and with that too many problems and I wasn't trying to be labeled as one of his hoes. He was a man who needed plenty of attention to be secure with himself; this was the reason he had so many women around him.

I met him at his house by eight o'clock as instructed and we headed out to the airport.

When we got out there we had to handle business first as always, we did our trade and we caught a cab to the dock where there was a private yacht waiting to take us to Key West.

"Wow this is really nice," I told him. "I wasn't quite expecting all of this."

"You can expect more things like this if you would just be my girl and stop playing games."

"Okay, let's just say I decide to be your girl, what happens to Veronica? She's in love with you; she sticks by your side no matter what type of shit you throw her way and Sharon done fell for you also. What happens to them?"

"Well if you don't want them around I will cut them off. They would just have to find them another leading man."

"Oh, it's just that simple huh?"

"Yeah, why wouldn't it be?"

We finally arrived in Key West. We had a beautiful suite that had everything we needed and it had two large beds a living room and a small kitchen. We changed into our swimming attire and laid out on the warm sand on the beach. We sipped on Mai Tais as we watched ocean and all of the beautiful people who walked by.

Later on that evening we got dressed into our evening attire and we headed out to Key West's finest club.

We were getting hammered; we had about five drinks a piece. Next thing I knew Chris, was popping one of those pills.

"Try one Cristina it ain't gonna kill you."

"No, are you crazy?" I asked him.

"Come on we're just having some fun that's all."

"Well, I don't want or need it. I'm high enough off these Mai Tais; the last thing I need to do is take a pill that I know very little to nothing about."

He got a bit angry but I didn't care. He shrugged his shoulders and he popped another one. He then started to get loud and he was now agitating me, so I went to the other side of the club.

I was on the dance floor dancing with some guy. The next thing I knew Chris was grabbing me by my arm and pulling me towards him. The guy looked pissed but luckily he didn't start anything. I wanted to cuss Chris out right then in there but I didn't want to cause a scene.

"What was that about?" I yelled out to him. "You just grabbed the shit out of my arm and you just embarrassed the hell out of me."

"My bad, I thought he was bothering you."

"Well you thought wrong. I'm tired and I'm ready to go back to the room. You don't have to come; I'm just exhausted, long day."

"Girl don't be silly I'm coming with you."

When we got back to the room I took a shower and changed into my pajamas and I hopped into bed. Next thing I knew this crazy motherfucker jumps in the bed with me butt naked. His dick was hard as a rock and as badly as I needed sex; I wasn't going to do it with him. No way, no how I was going to give him the satisfaction of saying he done fucked Sharon, Veronica, and me.

"What in the hell are you doing?" I yelled.

"What do you mean? I'm giving you what's long overdue"

"Oh no, I never said I was fucking you."

"What? You ain't stupid girl, you should have known this was coming. I done put plenty of money in your pockets, I could of got someone else to run my shit for way cheaper than what I was giving you. I know you hear me mentioning you and me being together all the time, and now we at the right place at the right time. You gonna give me some tonight!"

"You are drunk, and not in the right frame of mind, popping all them damn pills. Get the hell away from me and go to your bed. I will talk to you to tomorrow when you have better sense." He tried to climb on top of me once more and he sent me over the edge so I kicked him so hard in the stomach I sent him flying to the floor. The next thing I knew, his fist was flying towards my face.

"Oh no you didn't," I said as I got out of the bed and started packing all of my things.

"Where do you think you're going?" he said as he jumped up.

"I'm out of here you just put your hands on me and now I have a black eye."

"If you walk out of here you're done and I mean it. I may be drunk and high but I know when a bitch is using me. You playing games leading me on like there could potentially be something between us when really you never had intentions on being with me."

"You have two other girls living at your house right now as we speak and you're fucking both of them. Better yet y'all are all fucking each other. So who the fuck do you think you're playing, Go fuck yourself." I told him as I walked out the door. I took a cab to the airport and I took the next flight back to Los Angeles.

CHAPTER 10

The Joke's on me

When I got back to my new home I thought I would feel better but instead I felt alone. I had no friends, family, or a man around. I was all alone in this house.

I decided not to drown myself in my sorrows. I was going to try and make new friends by checking out Hollywood's nightlife.

I got dressed and I headed out to the club. I pulled up to valet and I headed to the front of a very long line. Everyone was eyeballing me, guys, and girls and I loved the attention. I walked up to the bouncer and I whispered some game into his ear: *"Baby if you let me pass all these people Ill put fifty dollars in your pocket right now."*

He thought about it for a second then he said, "Come on through, baby girl." I placed the money inside of his pocket. I heard all the girls in line fussing and cussing but I didn't care, I walked on past everyone and went on about my business.

I paid a few extra bucks to get into the VIP section and it was well worth it. I ordered a Grey Goose Cosmo and I studied everyone for a bit. Everyone was beautiful and everyone looked happy. After a few drinks I got up to dance. I wasn't dancing too hard or too soft, but I was dancing just right. I was dancing like I was making love to the music. I looked around and I saw a few guys eyeballing me.

I grabbed the guy who was wearing the glasses; he seemed to be watching me the most. I was going to be a good sport and dance with him like I was dancing with the finest nigga on earth. Doing this caught the attention of the other fellas. They probably wondered who was I and where did I come from. Soon enough they were all buying my drinks.

I all of a sudden noticed my target. He was a fine brother. He was tall, at least six feet. With muscular arms he was light skinned with dimples and normally I wasn't into light skinned guys but this one was fine and he had it going on from head to toe.

After I made my debut I decided to go back to my seat so that he could come and approach me. Less than thirty seconds later he was making his way over to my table.

"How are you this evening?" he asked me in one of the sexiest voices I'd heard yet. "By the way, I'm Darius, what's your name?"

"My name is Cristina."

"Can I buy you another drink?"

"No thanks, I think I'm way over my limit."

"So are you by yourself?" he asked.

"Yes, I just moved a couple of months ago and I thought I'd come out to check out Hollywood's night life since I heard so much about it, and I don't really need to bring a party, I am the party," I told him in my most confident voice.

"Well yeah I could see that, you got these guys eating right out of the palm of your hand, including me." He laughed. "Well, you look fabulous and I would be crazy to pass up a girl like you. I was hoping to get a chance to get to know you better."

"As fine as you are, hell yeah," I said as I grabbed my phone, I was ready to punch his number in my phone. After my talk with Darius I figured it was late and I should be headed home.

The next day I woke up to a frantic call from Sharon.

"Chrissie, you've got to help me, Chris just beat my ass. He blacked my eyes he bruised my body he pulled half of my hair out, girl you've got to help. I really need somewhere to stay." I was hesitant; I almost didnt trust her, hell, she could be trying to set me up for Chris for all I know but my heart told me to help her after all she was a person that I did consider a friend.

"Sure girl, you can stay over here." I gave her the address and she said she was on her way.

When I saw her face I was in shock. I know she said it was bad but it was a lot worse than I imagined.

"He tried to kill you." I told her as I examined her face.

"He's gone mad Chrissie, I'm telling you. Veronica was out with a trick one hour later than she was supposed to. When she came home he snatched the weave out of her head and he made her stay in her room for three days."

I hurried and got her an ice pack. "You can't ever go back there again, Sharon, you hear me? He's not in his right mind. He's been taking so many pills his brain is all messed up."

"He took at least four last night. I ran away in the middle of the night and to tell you the truth I'm scared; what if he finds me here?"

"Everything is going to be fine," I reassured her. "You just can't ever go back there."

"Chrissie, I got to tell you that he keep saying that he's going to get you and he keeps saying that you are a low-down dirty bitch. I'm so scared I don't know what he may try and pull. I say we stick together and leave this place and go back home to Bay area."

"But girl I just got this house and I just spent a lot of money furnishing it."

"I know Chrissie but our lives are more important than these material items."

Sharon did have a valid point and to be honest, I was now scared.

The next day I went and got an alarm system, two guns, and some pepper spray. I was going to be prepared for Chris if he was going to try to come my way.

Sharon and I were trying to map out a plan to get out of Los Angeles. I was convinced now more than ever that leaving would be the right thing to do.

The next day Sharon seemed down, as if she wasn't sure if leaving was the right thing to do.

"What's wrong?" I asked her.

"Everything's wrong with me. Chrissie, you have your whole life ahead of you when you get back home. You got money and a car you're beautiful and you're a natural leader. I got nothing just this same old car that I drove out here with. I don't have any friends or no real family. What am I going to do, go back to waitressing? When I came out here I felt like I had a life. I didn't mean to get involved in prostitution but it made me feel like I was wanted, like somebody needed me. Chris might be my only hope."

I looked at her as if she was the dumbest female on the whole planet earth. "Look at your face, look what he did to you. And besides, it was your idea to leave this place."

"I know, but I just been being hard-headed I haven't been following his instructions fully."

"That doesn't give him the right to put his hands on you, you're just making excuses for him. The reason why he's going crazy is because he keeps on taking them damn pills and they eating at his brain. What I think you need to do is take a nap and come back to reality."

A few hours later Chris called Sharon's cell phone. I didn't know what he was saying, but the look on her face told me that he was kissing her ass and she was loving every second of it.

"Let me guess: that was Chris right?"

"Yes, he was just calling to say that he's really sorry and that he really loves me and that he's going to do right by me this time. I also made him promise that he wouldn't do anything to you and he promised me he wouldn't, he said that he was out of line and he apologizes."

"Sharon, I can't believe you're falling for all this bullshit he's feeding you. Chris only cares for himself and he's never going to treat you like you deserve to be treated, he's never going to change. Sharon, I wish you could see that, he tried to run that same game on me telling me that he would get rid of you and Veronica, and that it was just going to be him and I. He is full of shit.

The expression on her face changed completely "Whatever Cristina, you're lying, you're just jealous because he wants me and not you."

"Jealous? Sharon please, I'm trying to let you know the truth about Chris; he ain't cool."

"You're full of shit, Chrissie, I'm gone."

"I know you got a brain in that head of yours, Sharon, use it!" I yelled.

"I'm gone," she said as she grabbed her bags and left my home.

I wasn't surprised. Sharon was the type of girl that would go back to a man after he beat the shit out of her, but she was a grown woman so I would have to let her see for herself that Chris was a no-good dog. And besides I didn't have time for someone else's drama; I had a hot date with Darius, the guy I met at the club the other night. There was one good thing from the situation; Sharon said that he'd promised her that he was no longer a threat to me.

Eight o'clock was here and I was ready for my date. I looked fabulous like always and my date was right on time, looking fabulous too.

"Hello pretty lady," he said as he grabbed my hand and he kissed it gently. He also handed me a fresh set of dozen roses.

He had a limo outside waiting, I also checked out his gear from head to toe and I counted at least ten thousand on him. If he didn't have my full attention before he do now, he had to be paid since he had a limo taking us on a simple date.

"What's up with the limo, do you always roll like that?"

"Whenever it's a special occasion and I consider our date a very special occasion."

He then had the driver to take us to a sushi restaurant.

"Oh, I'm sorry! I just took you to this restaurant and I didn't even ask you if you ate sushi or not."

"Are you kidding me, I love sushi, I know a lot of them ghetto chic's out there wouldn't, but I'm a little different." I said proudly.

"Well if you become my girl, I plan on us doing a lot of things, traveling to different places, trying out different types of foods. Those types of things. That's if you give a brother a chance. Do I even have a chance of being your man?" he asked.

"Yeah, I think you do," I said as I smiled. "I could picture myself being your woman one day. You're tall and handsome and you make a great date so far."

"So tell me a bit more about yourself?" I asked him.

"So what you want to know?"

"The basics what city were you born in, how many brothers and sisters do you have, who raised you? Those types of questions."

"I was born in Mississippi, I was raised by my grandma, my mom was on drugs and my dad died before I turned two."

"Wow, sounds a lot like my story, except my older sister raised me. Mom on drugs my dad was killed before I was born."

"I guess we have a lot in common then,"

"Yeah, I guess so," I had to admit Darius was a breath of fresh air.

After dinner he took me home and he kissed me softly kissed my cheek. I so badly wanted to invite him inside and give him some of my goods; I was long overdue for sex. But I didn't want him to think I was a slut, especially since I had a feeling that he was going to be the one. I went to bed dreaming about Darius.

I woke up the next day smiling to myself. I had found a potential Mr. Right and I was happy to have someone that I could hang out with around here. Darius was just what I needed, because I was almost on my way out of this town. He seemed to like me just as much as I liked him. He was the perfect gentleman, he had a good head on his shoulders, he could hold down an intelligent conversation and last but not least he was fine as hell. I was so happy when he told me that he wanted to go on a second date.

When he picked me up he had another set of roses for me. I put them in a vase and I sat them next to the other set of roses and I was ready to head out. He once again had limo service outside.

This time he took me to an upscale seafood restaurant in Hollywood. The restaurant was beautiful; the setting was perfect. We sat down at a small table made for two. He ordered us an expensive bottle of champagne and we ordered our entrees. I didn't know if it was the alcohol getting to me but he looked finer this time then he looked the last time and I wanted him so bad I could taste it. I kept telling myself to act like a lady and be patient and let him make the first move.

"So what did you say you do for a living again?" I asked him.

"I would consider myself an investor. I invest in a lot of different projects and I would say I've made some pretty good moves, business is going well. I own my own home, my two cars are paid for, I have a few dollars in my pocket and I have a few dollars invested, I'm just ready to settle down. I'm looking for that girl that I can spoil and take care of and hopefully that girl can be you."

He really had me smiling from ear to ear. Two hours had gone by. Our date was going really well and I wasn't quite ready for it to end.

"Do you want to continue this date somewhere else? I'm having so much fun and I just don't want it to end right now," he said.

"Sure I don't mind. I wasn't quite ready for it to end either."

"I know a place where I can rent a beautiful suite. We can order some champagne and some room service. I promise I won't try to have sex with you or make you uncomfortable in any way."

If only he knew that's what I wanted.

The suite had a Jacuzzi and a nice soft king sized bed. I knew that I was getting in that Jacuzzi no matter what. Darius ordered us some champagne and strawberries.

The service maid brought down a perfect setting of champagne in a bucket with chocolate covered strawberries.

I went in the bathroom and I got butt naked. I sprayed on a small amount of perfume and I pinned up my hair and I wrapped a fresh towel around my body. I knew that Darius wasn't going to be able to resist me.

When Darius saw me he looked in total shock.

"Wow, you don't have any clothes on under there, do you?"

"No, I don't," I said as I gave him a wink. I dropped my towel and I stepped inside the warm bubbling water. Darius had a glass of champagne with a strawberry inside of the glass waiting for me. We sipped champagne while he fed me strawberries.

I woke up butt naked in the bed in the suite. I turned around and looked at the clock; it read one o'clock pm. I then felt on the side of me and no one was there. I was feeling a bit strange and I knew that I couldn't be hung over; I'd only had a few glasses of champagne. I looked around for Darius. He wasn't anywhere in the suite. I called out for him a few times. There was no answer. I looked for my cell phone so that I could call him, but my phone was missing. I tried calling my phone from the phone that was in the room but the answering machine was coming on, on the first ring. I checked in my purse for the rest of my things. My wallet was gone along with my ATM cards and my thousand in cash. I then looked for my keys and they were gone. I was confused and I was still in a daze. I barely knew my way around this city and I didn't know where I was. At this moment I knew I had been drugged he must have put something in that glass of champagne. That was the last ting I remember. I threw on some clothes and I went downstairs to the lobby.

I started crying. "I need your help!" I told the lady at the front desk. "This guy that I came here with drugged me and he stole everything, he stole phone my wallet and he may have even raped me," I said as I sobbed. That bastard needed to be caught up with. He needed to pay for tricking me. I wasn't quite sure what his motives were but I sure in hell was about to find out. The lady tried to look up his name to see if she could get an address or some more info on him. But the name I gave her wasn't coming up; a different name was. The police said they would investigate it. I hoped the police would catch up with his trifling ass.

Now I had to call Mrs. Thompson, my landlord, because I couldn't get inside of my home. When I called her and explained what happen she was heated with me.

"Where have you been?" she yelled? "The house has been burned down to pieces; there's nothing left. Luckily for you I have fire insurance so you just have to pay for the deductible."

I couldn't believe it. I was in complete shock. I couldn't believe what Mrs. Thompson was telling me. My home with all of my clothes, my jewelry and my cash. Everything I owned was gone just like that.

"Mrs. Thompson, I am so sorry I didn't know. I've been in the hospital; I've been raped and drugged." I was hoping that she would feel some sympathy towards me.

"I knew that I shouldn't of have rented to you. In the back of my mind I knew you was trouble. That's my only property I own besides the one I live in, and I'm in a lot of debt myself so I would need you to pay the deductible."

I then hung up the phone. I was pissed off at how unsympathetic she was towards my situation. I finally made my way to the home,

Mrs. Thompson was right; the whole house was burned down
including my third Mercedes Benz. I couldn't believe that I had
gotten myself into this situation. My next run was to the bank. I
was in a nervous state. This was the only money that I had left to my
name. When I tried to withdraw my money, the banker confirmed
my worst fear. All of my money had been withdrawn from my
account. I just started acting a fool up in that bank.

"How in the hell do you let somebody come up in here that's
not even me and withdraw all my damn money? All of you need to
be fired."

"Well mam we would of never allowed it if the person didn't
have I.D."

Well that person wasn't me, is there any way I can get my money
today?"

"Sorry mam but we will have to do a full investigation."

"So what the hell am I suppose to do I the meantime?'

"I don't know I guess apply for aid." Said the women blankly.

I was in a helpless situation. I felt like I couldn't breath I wanted
to pass out. I started having a panic attack. I got so dizzy that I
passed out right in front of the bank.

I woke up to an older man helping me up. "Are you okay?" he
asked me.

"Yes," I said, still I was feeling dizzy.

"I'm going to get you to a hospital right away," he said as he
picked me up and he placed me in the car without me agreeing.

He drove off with me lying in the back seat of his car. I woke all
the way up and I came to my senses.

"Where are you taking me sir?" I asked him.

"To a hospital, sweetheart. You just passed out in front of that
bank."

"I don't need to go to a hospital. You can let me out right here."

He just kept on driving. He was completely ignoring me.

"Sir, did you hear what I said? You can let me out right here."

He kept on driving still ignoring me. I noticed he was pulling up to a very familiar home. It was Chris's home.

"Why in the hell did you take me here?" I yelled. I opened the door and I tried to run but the older man caught me. He was much stronger and faster than he looked. Chris came out with rope in his hands. They tied me up and they taped my mouth shut. They place me in one of the underground rooms. Then he slapped me in the face. Blood started pouring down my mouth and onto my shirt and I couldn't wipe it because my hands were tied. Then he walked out the door.

I was terrified. I didn't know what they had planned for me next. Six hours later Chris came down to feed me. He bought me four saltine crackers and some water.

"Why are you doing this to me?" I cried.

"Girl you are something else. You thought you were just going to make a couple of million dollars off of my connection and you was just gonna leave me and make me look foolish, you ain't know who you was fucking with!"

"I wasn't trying anything you were the one living it up doing your own thing having threesomes and shit. You couldn't possibly have been serious with me"

"Even if I was to be serious with you, you would have still played me. You're just that type of girl, you just pretend like you was half-interested in me while you collect money from my line. Then you run out on a nigga and you get you a home so you can probably share it with the next nigga. Damn, you low down and dirty." He then spit on my face and he walked out of the room. I knew that he hated me, I could hear the hatred in his voice and he probably was going to kill me or torture me or maybe both. I then flashed back on my life. I thought about how I was the most popular and prettiest girl in the school. There was no reason I should have stop going to school. I managed to make enemies with every single one of my friends. My mom and sister didn't even want to have anything to do with me. I knew I was wrong for staying around Chris and leading him on, knowing that I was only around to get paid. The sad part about it is that I had a good amount of money of my own. But instead I wanted to be greedy and it looked like I would pay the ultimate price: my life.

Four hours later Chris came back down. He then snatched off all of my clothes and he pulled his pants down and he entered me from behind. He was being extra rough. It felt like he was tearing up my insides.

"You wish you would have just gave me some that night now, huh?" He yelled out while still pushing himself in and out of me; he was using all of his strength and I felt he was ripping me apart. Huge watermelon tears rolled down my bright red cheeks. I was so scared. I could tell he was losing it by the second and I didn't know what to expect next. I was hurting so bad and I was now bleeding. All of a sudden he pulled out and he squirted his cum all over my face and hair.

"That's going to stay there," he yelled out. He then left me in the room. I was tied up butt naked with semen all over my face and hair.

"How did I get myself into this?" I kept asking myself. I had hit rock bottom. I had not even two cents to my name. I had no car, no clothes, and no jewelry. My hair was disgusting. My private parts were sore with dried up blood all around. At this point I wanted to die. I just wanted all of this to end.

When he came back down he placed me in the shower and he helped washed me down since he kept me handcuffed.

"How come you just don't kill me?" I blurted out.

"I have plans for you my dear," was all he said.

"Can you please kill me and get it over with," I cried to him.

"Shut up, I'm getting real sick and tired of hearing your mouth. You ain't nothing but a gold digging stuck up little bitch who thinks who thinks to highly of themselves." "Now look at you. You looked all fucked up now, that's what the hell you get for being a Bitch."

"What do you want with me? For crying out loud just kill me and get it over with."

"Shut up with all of that whining," he said as he backhanded me right in my face. He then went back up the stairs. When he came back down he had Sharon with him.

"Oh my God she cried. " Why did you do her like this? You said you wouldn't hurt her, what's wrong with you?"

"Shut up before you're next, I really don't trust any of you hoes Matter fact for yelling at me, I got a treat for you."

Sharon got really scared.

"Take off your clothes"

She was confused. She didn't know what to think but she obeyed him and she took off her clothes.

"You supposed to be my bitch and you over here defending her trifling ass. She tried to pull a fast one on your man and you sit there and feel sorry for her?"

Sharon wasn't moving quickly enough because he backhanded her in the face.

"I said take off your clothes," he barked.

Sharon started undressing immediately.

He looked over at me "Now for you low down dirty bitch, I'm about to make you do something you said you would never do."

"Sharon, lay back and spread your legs."

I instantly knew what this fool was trying to make me do. I cringed at the thought of it.

"No," I said as I shook my head.

"Oh yeah, yeah, get down there right now and lick her pussy."

By now Sharon was crying; she couldn't believe Chris was humiliating us in this way.

I guess I wasn't moving fast enough because he pulled out a pistol from out of his back pocket. He fired twice in the ceiling leaving more tears in our eyes.

"I said do it," he grew increasingly inpatient.

"I'd rather die first," I cried.

"I will torture the shit out of you. I'm crazy right now so you better do what I say," he said as he grabbed me by my neck and forced my head in between Sharon's legs.

"Lick it, kiss it, do something to it."

"Just do it," cried Sharon softly. I took a deep breath and closed my eyes and I did what he asked. I tried my hardest to block what I was doing out my mind but I couldn't. He grabbed himself a chair and he watched as he jacked himself off.

When he released himself he told me that was enough.

Still sobbing, Sharon put on her clothes and ran up the stairs.

"And my boy Darius got you good. My plan worked like a charm. I knew your gold digging self was going to fall right into the trap. I told you I would get you one way or another. Now you're fucked. You don't have a cent to your name. Darius, Sharon and I cleaned you out and now you're in debt. I got you to lick a pussy. Your life is ruined; I told you that you didn't know who you were fucking with."

"I know, so please, just kill me. You've humiliated me enough."

"Killing you would be too easy and there's no way I can let you go now. You could put me away forever. Let's see, kidnapping and rape, that's twenty-five alone and not counting everything else. So you're never going home; you can forget about that. You gonna be my sex slave for now." He left out the room leaving me in the dark. The thought of being his sex slave for the rest of my life was sickening to my stomach. I knelt down and got on my knees and I prayed to the Lord. I hadn't had a conversation with God in a long time and it's sad to say that I only called out to him now that I was in deep trouble.

"Dear God, I know that I have been a horrible person. I know that I've been rude, stuck up and self-centered, a manipulator, a liar and a home wrecker. I'm not very proud of myself and I know you're disappointed in me. I just wanted you to know that I've been really thinking about my actions and I know that if I wasn't always trying to use people, I probably wouldn't be in this position right now. Chris said he's never letting me go home. I know I haven't treated my mom and my sister that good, but I really miss them and I would give anything to see them one last time. I also miss my nephew and my brother-in-law and I really miss Trey and I also miss Katrina and Carmen. I wish that I could see them once more; I would show them a different me. I promise God if you get me out of this one, I will change my life around and I would devote myself to you, I promise."

I sat in a fetal position. I wiped the tears from my eyes with my knees since my hands were still tied. I silently rocked myself back in forth until I feel asleep.

The next morning I was awoken by loud noises. I heard some guys entering the house. I immediately grew scared. I then heard some tussling. Then I heard Chris scream at the top of his lungs, "Please don't kill me." I then heard about ten gunshots. A few seconds later I then heard Sharon screaming help from the top of her lungs I then heard if you don't be quiet, we'll kill you to. Sharon kept screaming for help and moments later I heard a few more gunshots. I felt l like I was going to have a nervous breakdown. I then heard the guys leave out the door. I let out a sigh of relief but I still was in a nervous wreck.

Twenty minutes later I heard someone coming toward the door. "Oh shit," I said to myself.

Veronica came in the room acting as if nothing happened.

"What's going on? I heard gunshots," I was still shaking uncontrollably.

"Calm down," she said as she grabbed the knife. I first thought she was going to try and kill me but to my surprise she untied the ropes. By now I was even more confused. "Where's Chris?" I finally asked.

"He's dead," she said calmly. It was clear she was unfazed by it. She was now searching the basement like a maniac. She stopped searching when she came across a box. When she opened it she pulled out a key. She pulled back the carpet in the corner and she pulled out a safe. She used the key to open it. Inside were stacks and stacks of cash.

I then went upstairs and I saw Chris and Sharon's dead bodies lying on the floor. I was so happy I was free, but the reality set in when I saw my friend lying on the floor dead.

Veronica came back up the stairs with two duffel bags.

"I know I gave you a hard time and all. But I still don't think you deserved all the fucked up shit Chris did to you. He deserved to die. He thought he was running me but I had him fooled. You see he fucked over the wrong dudes. He scammed them for five million and they wanted him dead. They then approached me to help them get inside the house and they would give me half the money. They put all these things in my head, that Chris didn't give a fuck about me and that I better start looking out for me. At first I declined. I was down with Chris real tough. I loved him and I guess it was just wishful thinking that one day he would stop messing around and only be into me. He did so much shit to me. He called me stupid bitch all the time, he called me a drug prostitute, but it was his fault I was on drugs and I was prostituting for him to make a better life for us. I didn't tell anybody, but a couple of months back I was pregnant. When I gave him the news he whooped my ass so badly I lost the baby. I never looked at him the same since. My love for him took a turn for the worse. Then when the same men approached me again I was down. I wanted him dead. He didn't deserve to live after he beat my baby out of me."

"As far as Sharon goes I would say she over stepped her boundaries. She tried to have a real relationship with Chris under my nose like I didn't know what was going on. Bad move on her part."

"That doesn't give you the right to have her killed.'

"You feel bad for her? She's the one who use your I.D. and

cleaned out your bank account. She was a fake ass female who tried to act like she liked me but was plotting against me the whole time. You on the other hand never liked me and you never pretended to either, now that, I can respect.

"Chris had three places where he kept his money. One he never told me about and I still don't know about. He kept another safe up in his room, which had eight million. The men got four million and I got four million. That was how we were splitting the money. I didn't tell them that there was another safe in the basement which had another eight million, so you see, I am the ultimate winner."

I was surprised, I didn't know Veronica had it in her to pull off such a scheme. She then threw me a bag and said. "You will probably need this, I heard Chris milked you dry."

I stood there looking confused but if there was one thing she was right about was that I needed the money.

"We better get out of here before the cops come." We both ran our separate ways.

CHAPTER 11

Caught Up

I stopped at the nearest hotel. I needed to get myself together, I needed to take a shower and get cleaned up and plan my next move. I needed to count the money to see how much Veronica gave me.

I took a shower and washed my hair. My body was still sore from all the foul shit Chris had done to me. After I came out the shower I added up all the cash she left with me. I counted a little over 50,000.00 dollars. Even though I know she had gotten away with a whole lot more. I was satisfied because she could have killed me or even gotten me killed and she could have left me with nothing.

The more I started to add things up in my head the more paranoid I became. I had just left a home where a double murder had taken place. I contemplated back and fourth should I have called the police or not. Especially since one of the victims was my friend. I started to feel bad that I'd just left her there. I left the crime scene with a bag of money in my hand. I didn't think about how morally wrong I was or the fact that someone may have spotted me.

I came up with a quick plan: I was going to get a couple of

outfits, some food, my hygiene needs and keep only six thousand on me. I was going to western union my sister the rest When I called I could tell she was still upset. Sabrina was good for holding grudges. I basically forgot about why everything got so blown up.

"Sabrina, I really need your help. I need to send you forty three thousand I need you to hold on to that for me until I get things together."

"Get what together Cristina? What is going on?"

"Long story, I just need you to accept the money and Ill explain things later.'

"Ok sure she said"

"Got to go, love you sis sorry for everything, I said as I hung up."

Later that evening when I got back from getting some of my needs, the news did more than just surprise me; it scared the shit out me. Not only was the double homicide the first thing on, Veronica's and my picture were on the screen. They said neighbors spotted us running from the crime scene a little after they heard gunshots. They also said they had two men already in police custody.

"Oh my god," I kept saying to myself. I got to do something. I stopped by the corner store and bought some red hair dye. I made it back just in time to watch the late night news. They were saying how they already had caught up to Veronica and she was caught with millions of dollars on her.

Truth was, they *had* caught up to the right person. She was behind the murder's she helped set it up, not me. But what scared me most is that I know she didn't like me and she could blame the whole thing on me. Now the police were looking for me and I had nothing to do with any of this shit. Veronica had handed me a bag of money and me not having a dollar to my name, I took it. Something told me she had something up her sleeve.

I went to the bathroom and chopped my hair off, I gave myself a short bob, which I dreaded, but I knew it would grow back fast. I then dyed it a bright red color. This look definitely wasn't me but it was going to have to do for now. I then packed my bags and I left in the middle of the night to the Greyhound bus station. I purchased a one-way ticket to Seattle, Washington.

I sat at the stop with layers of clothing on and I had on a hoodie. I was definitely trying to hide my appearance. When I got to the ticket clerk I was scared because she studied the shit out of my I.D. I also noticed the guards watching me very closely. I didn't know what to do. A part of me wanted to run out of the station but the other part of me was thinking that I was being extra paranoid. I knew I needed to stay and get on the bus to Seattle and lay low for a while. I needed to gather my thoughts find a good lawyer to get me out of this bullshit.

It was finally time to get on the bus after an hour in a half long wait. When the bus took off I felt ten times better.

A day later, the bus arrived in Seattle. When I got off the bus I got inside a cab.

"Where are you headed?" ask the driver in his Indian accent.

"Can you take me to a Hotel please?"

"Sure no problem, "said the cab driver as he kept driving.

As soon as the cab driver pulled up to the hotel I saw police everywhere.

"Put your hands up," yelled out the officers.

I instantly threw my hands in the air; my heart was beating so fast it felt like it was about to jump out of my chest. An officer than came and slapped hand cuffs on me on site.

CHAPTER 12

Locked Up

I later found out they were on my ass every since I showed my I.D. at the bus station. Jail was everything and more than what I pictured it to be. It was dirty, cold and hella manly ass females.

I made my first free call to my sister. I couldn't believe she sound cool. I thought she would be screaming her head off. I could tell she was pissed off at me and she was holding back. I knew she wanted to let me have it. Especially since all she ever tried to do was help me. She tried to school me and instead of listening to what she was saying I accused her of being a hater.

"Chrissie," she said softly. I could tell she was trying to maintain her composure. "What in the hell did you get yourself into, Why did you send me that money, Whats going on?"

"I don't know sister, I am so sorry. I know that all you ever tried to do was help me and I know I screwed up. I just hope you have some trust in me. You gotta believe me that I am not guilty of what they're accusing me of."

"Well Chrissie, I know that you may be a lot of things, but I know you're not a murderer. Mom and I already done hired one of the best attorneys in law to help get you off. So tell me this sis, how are you holding up in there?"

"Not so well to be honest. I know I try to be tough and all, but I'm not cut out for this shit. These bitches are ruthless and crazy and, I haven't touched a bite of my food."

"Just hold on tight baby sis, me and moms got your back."

I needed that talk. She just gave me some hope because I was starting to think there wasn't any.

I decided to write my mom. I really needed to get some things off my chest.

> Dear Mom,
>   I am deeply sorry for all of the pain I caused you. I really don't know what's gotten into me over the last few years. I guess I took full advantage of the situation. I knew how you felt about all the hell you put me through during my younger years. But I never really tried to fully understand your position. You were a single mother with a newborn baby when your husband got murdered. You were in a tough place, and God has blessed you because you overcame it and you're a great mother now. I really wish I would have known Dad. I hear you and Sabrina say all these great things about him and I wish I had gotten a chance to get to know him. Maybe that's why I've been acting out messing around with older men, maybe I needed that father figure. But I know if Dad looking down on me he can't be proud of me. I feel like I let everyone down. If God get me out of this I'm vowing to change my life around. I bought some stamps with the money that you and Sabrina put on my books so I will be writing to you as often as I can. Now I must sit in

this jail cell and await my fate, whatever happens to
me at the end of the day, I want you to know that
I love you Mom.

Love,
Your daughter Cristina

Later on that evening in the cafeteria we were all having dinner.
I noticed this woman kept looking my way. She was making me feel
slightly uncomfortable. I was trying to figure out what in the hell
she wanted. She then started to walk my way.

"Is your name Cristina Brown?" she asked.

"Yeah, that's my name, why you wanna know?" I asked her.

"I know you probably don't remember me; the last time I saw
you, you were practically a baby, but I'm your cousin Nikki. I
recognized you because you look like a spitting image of your sister."

"Oh, so you're Nikki, I done heard all about you," I told her.

"I'm sure you've heard some not-so-very-good things, especially
if it was coming out of Sabrina's mouth."

"You were sleeping with her man in their home, what do you
expect? But hey, I'm a big girl, I can judge people for myself."

"I can see you different from Sabrina already, but my question
to you is what's your little ass doing in here?"

"Look, I done got caught up into some bullshit that I didn't even
have anything to do with, and what're you in here for?"

"Some bullshit charges really, I was messing around with
Michael and I got caught up in his operation; they gave me a few
years but I get out soon though, I may have needed this, I have a
clear head and I've been alcohol and drug free for some time now.

"Michael, yeah I done heard all about him too."

"I'm sure your sister told you everything."

"Yes she did, and that you and Michael were off the chain." I laughed. "I don't know how you survive in here, I've only been in here for a few days and I'm freaking out."

"Well since you're my little cousin you don't worry about anything. My girlfriend is the H-B-I-C, the head bitch in charge. She runs this joint. She's running an operation in Miami as we speak. She's got folks lining up mad money on her books and if you down with us ain't nobody gonna fuck with you up in here."

Now I'd seen Peaches around; she was Puerto Rican and she was about 5'6. She wore her long hair in cornrows going down the back and she looked like she could be a pretty woman if she'd wanted to, but she was much too hardcore for that. She had a couple of chicks that were trying to be on her team. But of course she wanted Nikki. Nikki had to be in her mid thirties but she was still beautiful as ever and her breast and ass was still in place just as if she was in her early twenties. It didn't surprise me that Nikki was messing around with a chick. My sis told me all about her crazy ass, she describes her as being a tri-sexual, meaning that she'll just about try anything.

"So just let me know if you need me, cousin. Be seeing you around," she said, and then she went to join her lover.

When I got back to my cell there was a letter waiting for me to read. I opened it and it read.

> Dear Cristina,
>
> I know I am probably the last person you expected to hear from. I just wanted to come clean about a few things. I just wanted to apologize for leaving you stuck that day. My ex-wife and I were going through some pretty heavy issues. She had gotten a hold of all my money in all of my accounts she found out I bought that car for you and she wiped me clean out. I swear I wanted to come back for you. But at the time she held the cards and I had to play by her rules. I know that I should have

been straightforward. But there's one thing that I am certain of is that I loved you and I'm still in fact in love with you. When I saw you on the news I was shocked. I couldn't believe all of the trouble you got yourself into. A part of me feels like it's all my fault. I feel if I was there for you like I should have been you would've never gotten into this mess. I will make it up to you. I will hire you a great attorney. I know you're innocent. Please write me back.

Take care of yourself,
Love, Sam

I was completely blown away. He had nerve to be writing me, and nerve for trying to apologize for all that bullshit he pulled. I didn't want to hear anything he had to say. I didn't need him or his attorney's help. I decided that I wasn't going to respond. He should have been up front with that same story long ago. And there's one thing I agreed upon: if he would never have let me down like he did, and if he would have done everything like he promised, I probably wouldn't even be in this predicament.

I placed the letter in the trash and I fell asleep fantasizing about getting out of this place.

As I was in my bed reading a magazine my name was being called for visiting. I tried to fix my hair as best as I possibly could; I wasn't trying to look all grimy. I saw that it was some white man in an expensive suit awaiting me.

"Hello Ms. Brown," he said, as he reached out his hand. "My name is Mr. Perkins; I will be handling your case for you. Now let's get down to business," he said as he pulled out his paperwork.

"Looks like you're in here for accessory to murder. The police aren't convinced that you were the actual perpetrator but they are convinced you had something to do with the planning of it. The police said they found ten thousand on you. Your sister said that you had inherited way more than that from your deceased father. So that's a plus if that can be proven. And as far as the evidence goes, they have two witnesses, the neighbors. They said they saw you and Veronica Sanchez running from the scene. I'm guessing Ms. Sanchez is not too fond of you. She's blaming everything on you. She's saying that you had two guys kill Christopher Bailey and Sharon Cark. So tell me your side of the story."

"That bitch," I said to myself. "Mr. Perkins, I had nothing to do with the murder. Chris kidnapped me. He tortured me and raped me and had me held down in the basement. It was the second day of being in the basement I heard loud commotions going on then I heard gunshots. I was in fear of my life; I thought that I would be next. I heard the guys leaving and then I feared that no one would ever find me and I was going to die in that basement. Veronica came down a little while later. I knew she didn't care for me so I thought she was going to kill me but to my surprise she let me free. And I know you're probably wondering why I didn't go to the police. I didn't want to go through more drama. I just wanted to get away as far as I could and its not like I could have been a good witness because technically I didn't see anyone get killed.

When Mr. Perkins examined my arms I knew that he knew that I was a victim, still I know that he questioned my involvement with the murder.

"So how close were you and the other victim, Ms. Clark?"

"She and I were friends. I would have never had her killed. She was actually a really sweet girl. I really can't believe Veronica's blaming everything on me. She's the one who told me how and why she set up Chris and Sharon to get killed, and how did they get a hold of Veronica so fast?"

"They caught the two hit men first. They were pulled over an hour after it happened; they led police on a high-speed chase. When they searched the vehicle it had the murder weapon and hardcore cash, I believe over four million. They searched the men's cell phones and found numerous calls made to Ms. Sanchez's phone. They caught up with Ms. Sanchez and she claimed she got the millions from Chris and that he loved her and that she would never kill him.

Well Cristina, you have some things going in your favor. The police didn't find a whole lot of money on you. Number two, the two men said they don't know who you are but they recognized Ms. Sanchez. The bad thing is you didn't go to the police. And you were his victim so you have a motive to kill Chris. I'm going to be honest with you Cristina this is going to be a hard case to beat."

I didn't like hearing that, but I just hoped and prayed that he was as good as my sister claimed him to be. Now I knew why Veronica was so quick to let me free and had given me all that cash. She was preparing to set me up since I had a motive to kill Chris. I just hoped this lawyer knew what he was doing. I didn't tell him every single detail. I couldn't tell him the real reason I didn't call the police is because I wanted in on that money.

The next morning I had received another letter. It read:

Dear Cristina,

I know that you're probably upset with me. I just wanted you to know that you've been on my mind since the day you left. I feel like I've been a selfish man. I was feeling you from the jump; I always had a thing for you, I just didn't know how to express myself and of course I had a few concerns. You were a hand full, and I just didn't know what to do with a girl like you.

Another thing I wanted to clear up, I told you that another chick was coming down to stay with me. I made that story up because I grew scared. I was falling in love with you. I know in my heart you're innocent. I feel like this is my fault in a way. I hope you can forgive me some day. I feel like I screwed up. But I've come to my senses. I just hope it's not too late. I'm going to put some money on your books and let me know if I could visit you.

Love always, Trey

P.S. I hope and pray that you still carry those same feelings for me.

I didn't mean to overreact but as soon as I read the letter I jumped up and down like I had just won the lottery. That quick, I had forgotten I was in jail fighting a huge case. I instantly took out my pad in pen; I needed to write him to tell him all about what's been going on with me.

Dear Trey,
You have no idea how happy I was to receive a letter from you. I even got a little teary eyed. I don't want you to feel bad because it was you who warned me about Chris in the first place. I was hardheaded and I had to learn things the hard way. But to make a long story short I am completely innocent; I just got caught up in some bullshit and I hope justice prevails. I'm doing okay in this hellhole. It isn't too bad. I got my cousin and her peeps in here just in case some shit pops off. I got money on my books to get my necessities. I'm reading a lot and I'm trying my best to stay out of drama. I also wanted to tell you that if you and God give me the chance of being your woman, I would do whatever it takes to

keep you happy. Pray for me and pray that I make
it home.

Love always, Cristina

At lunch I spotted Nikki and her girlfriend. They were sitting
with a couple of their other friends. One girl in particular kept
looking at me. Nikki walked over to the table where I was sitting.

"Hey cousin, I see that you're in a good mood, spill the beans!"

"My long time crush just wrote me a letter and he's the last
person I thought I'd hear from. He sort of caught me by surprise."

"Awwh that's good but I came over to tell you some news,
Peaches' best friend Loca has a mad crush on you."

"I see her keep looking over here like she want to eat me, and so
what you telling me for? I don't swing that way."

"Girl if you got a lot of time to do you better hook up with her.
I'm telling you she got mad cash. She rolls with my boo and they
getting big money on the outside right now as we speak."

"Well hopefully by the grace of God I will get off free since I'm
innocent."

"So you ain't gonna at least entertain her while your here?" she
asked once more.

"No, I mean hell no, first off what kind of name is Loca? Ain't
that supposed to mean crazy in Spanish? The last thing I need to
do is mess with some female named Loca." I said as I laughed. Even
the thought of that was funny. I don't have anything against y'all in
all but I'm cool I just need to stay focused and out of the drama."

"Okay, I tried to hook you up with some security, with money
and protection."

"Well thank you anyway, big cuz, but I got this."

Later on that evening we were let out for dinner and I noticed
another female looking me up and down. I tried to pay her no
attention but it was like she wanted me to notice her, she wanted

me to say something to her. She saw that I wasn't feeding into her plan so she then got up and bumped into me and it wasn't a soft bump either.

"Excuse you," I said loudly. "What the hell is your problem?" By now I was pissed. I was sick and tired of these bitches in here fucking with me over little shit.

"I hear you was trying to get with my baby Loca!"

"Loca, the chick who was trying to get with me? I don't want your girl or none of these girls or a girl period."

"Yeah right, all I know is you better stay away from my girl."

"Look bitch, I done told you, I don't want your girl, she wanted me. Now you better get the fuck out my face before I kick your ass."

Next thing I knew she threw a punch at me and it was on from there. We were boxing all over the cafeteria, the guards finally broke us up and we both got thrown in the hole. Everything happened so fast that when I thought about what this fight could do to my case, it was too late. I was disappointed by the fact that I didn't ignore the girl, but I was pushed to my limit. There were way too many females in this place for me. I was sick and tired of this place straight up.

CHAPTER 13

On Trial

*J*was more than nervous on my first day of trial. I knew that if they
brought up the fight that I had last night it would hurt my case
a great deal. On the way to court, I thought about who would be at
my hearing. I didn't want Trey showing up. I didn't want him seeing
me like this. I still was good looking even in my jail uniform. It's
just I didn't want him to see me handcuffed looking like a criminal.

When it was my turn to face the judge and the jury I was
shaking in my boots. I examined the courtroom and I saw my moms
and sister and my brother-in-law Jay on one side. When I looked on
the other side I saw Sam in the middle row and then I spotted Trey
in the back row. "Damn, everyone is here," I said to myself.

"Ms. Cristina Brown how do you plea?" asked the judge.

"Not guilty," I said knowing that I was taking a huge risk. If
the jury found me not guilty I would be set free. And if I was found
guilty I would be facing twenty-five to life. I was sick to my stomach
at the thought of staying in this place that long of a time.

I looked at the jury trying to give them an innocent face. I
wanted them to see that I wasn't a murderer.

The D.A. was a woman named Charlene Franklin. She looked like she was going to try to eat me alive. She was a sista; she was brown skinned and tall. Her presence alone was very powerful. I could tell she took all of her cases very seriously especially by the way she kept studying her notes.

She preceded her case by saying, "Your Honor and Jury, Cristina Brown may look like she's sweet and innocent, but I assure you she isn't. She was also seen running from the crime scene. If she wasn't involved like she says why didn't she call the authorities? Things just don't add up if you ask me."

I sat in the courtroom for a couple of hours listening to all this bullshit that was being said about me. I wanted to cuss this woman out so bad and tell her that she didn't know me or shit about me. But there was no way I could. She tried to paint a picture of me being a troubled kid because my mom was on drugs and I grew up without a father and I was sent to a group home. She also brought up the fight that I had with Loca's girlfriend.

I left the court devastated, knowing that she had grabbed the attention of the jury by painting a very nasty picture of me. The worst part of it all was that my lawyer seemed as if Ms. Franklin intimidated him.

She'd done more homework on me than he and I both expected.

I told him he better do something; he was getting paid damn good.

When I got back in this hard ass thing they called a bed, I started to have a full on panic attack. I laid there crying; I wasn't able to stop the tears from falling. I couldn't picture this being my home for the next twenty-five years. I would rather die. Right now all I wanted to do was call my mom or sister or someone who would listen to me vent. But I couldn't just pick up the phone when I wanted to. I was sick of using the bathroom in front of my cellmate. I was sick of taking showers in front of these bitches. I was sick of looking at all these bitches period. I had finally reached my breaking point.

A week later I had received more letters from Sam and Trey. I wondered why Sam was being so persistent. I figured he and his wife must have separated. I opened Sam's letter first, not that I cared about anything he had to say.

> Dear Cristina,
>   I hope all is well. I hope you don't still hate me. I see you didn't respond to my first letter. All I ask for you is to not shut me out and at least hear what I have to say. I know that I'm in love with you and only you. I came to your court hearing and I must say I was a little disappointed in your lawyer for not speaking up for you like he should. I really think my lawyer can help you. Ms. Franklin painted a pretty ugly picture of you. I know the real you and I know that you're innocent. I hope that one day you can forgive me and understand where I'm coming from. My dream is for us to one day be together. Please let me know if there's anything you need. I miss you dearly, id give anything to hold you in my arms once more.
>
> Love always, Sam

Sam must of thought I was so stupid the returning address was his work place; he had to still be with his wife because he didn't want me sending a letter to his house. Even though it didn't matter I wasn't going to write him back anyway. I waited to open the best one for last. I took a deep breath and I opened the letter from Trey, It read:

Dear Cristina,

Hello baby girl, I know court didn't go as
expected. Your sister, mom, Jay and I are pushing
Mr. Perkins to do his best to beat this case. I will
be devastated if you lose. I hope you keep your head
up for now and stay strong, even though I can't tell
you how to feel because I couldn't possibly imagine
how you must feel inside. I keep asking myself over
and over why I ever let you leave in the first place. If
you lose your case I know that I would never forgive
myself. If God answers my prayers and brings you
home safely. I promise you I will make it up to you.

Love always, Trey
P.S. Keep your head up lil mama!

I almost shed a tear but instead I got on my knees. I asked the
Lord to please forgive me for all my wrong. I also asked him to please
let me be with the love of my life.

When my court date came around again, I was extremely
nervous. This was the day that determined my fate. When I got to
the court I was shaking in my boots. I looked around and I saw my
mom sister and Jay and Trey and Sam once again.

Ms. Franklin looked fully energized and ready to take me down.
She made me even more nervous because she had a smirk on her face
like she had the case in the bag.

Ms. Franklin then went on to proceed with her case. "The
defendant looks innocent and sweet, but the evidence is clear. She
was running from a crime scene. Why else would she be running
if she weren't guilty? If she had no involvement like she claims, she
would have done the right thing and called the police, especially
since she calls Ms. Clark a friend, instead she ran away from the

scene and she did not look back. I don't know what kind of a friend would ever leave their friend dead. Now ladies and gentlemen of the jury, she sounds guilty to me. I hope that you find it in your hearts to know the truth and give justice to Christopher Bailey and Sharon Clark's family, so their hearts can start healing, I rest my case," she said as she sat down smiling.

At this point I was ready to give up. The fact that I didn't go to the police made me look guilty and ultimately I knew that would hurt my case the most. I looked over at my mom and sister. My mom had tears coming down her cheeks. I almost started to cry but I knew I had to hold it in.

My lawyer got out of his chair. He stood up with confidence. It seemed like all of his lights had suddenly come on.

"Well, you see here ladies and gentlemen. My client's cell phone was reported missing; she had no cell phone. On the other hand Ms. Sanchez made over thirty out going phone calls to the defendant. Blaming the whole thing on my client is ludicrous. My client didn't have her phone for days, which supports her story that Christopher kidnapped her.

Her phone, purse, makeup and I.D. were all found in Christopher's bedroom.

Christopher held her down in the basement. Forensics found hair follicles in one certain area where he kept her captive.

Now, don't you think if she helped plan a murder she would have grabbed her phone and wallet? I know you may have questions or doubts about why didn't she call the police. She was scared and besides, her kidnapper was already dead. He was killed because he was a bad man. The evidence clearly shows he was involved with a selling a whole lot of drugs; he was involved with big time dope dealers. The man had enemies. He got what was coming to him. He was a bad guy.

And last but not least the two hit men claim they don't know and have never seen my client. The evidence is clear: Veronica and the hit men planned this on their own and my client had nothing to do with this. I hope you the jury do what's right and find my client not guilty."

I was impressed. Mr. Perkins sure did put up a good argument and after all he did go all out to fight my case.

It was now time for the jury to deliberate and I was nervous as hell. Mr. Perkins did put up a great fight but Ms. Franklin put up a great fight as well. I didn't know which way the jury would go.

A few hours later the jury was done deliberating; it was now time to announce the verdict. They all stood up and one person spoke for them all.

"We the jury find the defendant not guilty of all charges."

I couldn't believe what I was hearing, I wanted to jump up and down but I knew it would be inappropriate. I gave Mr. Perkins the biggest hug and kiss.

"Thanks for all your hard work," I said softly. I then ran to my sister and mother and hugged them. We all jumped up and down. I then saw Trey and Sam. They both had their arms out for me to hug them. I ran right into Trey's big strong arms. It felt so good to be in Trey's arms and he had a tight grip on me as if he never wanted to let me go.

I looked over at Sam. He had a evil look on his face.

"So is he the only person you see? Is this the dude you were chasing while you were with me?" Sam asked.

"Look Sam that's none of your business. You belong with your wife. What we had is over." He looked as if he was about to blow up. But instead he took a deep breath and said to me in a calm voice, "This ain't over," and he walked out of the courtroom.

Later on that day I was discharged from jail and I promised Nikki that I was going to stay in touch.

I almost couldn't believe this moment. I was free to go home and Trey was outside waiting for me.

CHAPTER 14

New Beginnings

Two years later, Trey and I were married and we had a baby girl named Adrianna. I never imagined myself married with a kid at twenty-years-old. I have no regrets I loved my new life and a man didn't come no better than Trey in my eyes. I had a precious baby girl. She looked like a spitting image of me when I was a small. Adrianna was getting to be a real handful at one-years-old but we were all enjoying her.

I also took up cosmetology, and I got my license and opened up a salon called Sassy's, the same name of the salon my mother had when I was a baby, before the drugs.

Moms was real proud of me and so was my sister and it meant a lot getting their approval, especially Sabrina's.

Trey still owned the carwash and he had his mind set upon opening three more in the Bay Area. We bought a huge house right next door to my sister.

I eventually made up with Katrina and Carmen. We were young and stupid. I had no business blowing up over a material item and eventually she realized she had no business letting her boyfriend at the time drive my car. I now felt complete. I had my daughter, husband, mother, sister, Mrs. Jenkins, and friends.

I kept in touch with Mrs. Jenkins. She was like a Grandmother to me. She went from living in the hospital to living in a senior citizen's home. She was doing quite well on her own. She felt most comfortable being independent.

My sister and mom kept my trial a secret from Mrs. Jenkins. They didn't want anything upsetting her, especially since she had been doing extremely well. We all go up to her place and visit her from time to time. My mom had this wonderful idea to throw a surprise party for Mrs. Jenkins' seventy-fifth birthday. We were all running around like chickens with our heads cut off, making the last runs for the party. There were still lots of things that needed to be done. I still needed to go to the party warehouse to pick up decorations and I still needed to go to the bakery to pick up the cake, but first I had a few clients that I needed to finish.

When I pulled up to the salon I saw Sam parked out in front of the parking lot. He caught me off guard. The last time I saw him was two years back when he was saying, "This ain't over."

"What are you doing here?" I asked him.

"Why are you treating me like this? I remember you used to really love me once upon a time, I miss you like crazy, I can't seem to get over you."

"You know what I think; I think you done lost your forever-loving mind. You need to let things go. I'm a whole different person then I used to be. I'm married now and I have a family. I strongly suggest you leave me alone and attend to yours. Now get out of here before I call the police." I walked toward my salon.

"It was okay to sleep with me when I was married, but you don't want me messing up your family, some nerve," he said. He stood there for a second and then I noticed he had a look his eyes, a look which I had never seen before in him. Then he politely got in his car and drove off.

After I finished my clients it was time for me to head to the bakery to pick up the cake. On my way to the bakery I took some time out to reflect on what happened earlier. I thought that maybe I should have called the police anyway, just in case anything was to go down. They would have it documented. I then called Trey so I could let him know about Sam coming to my salon.

I was hoping Trey wouldn't overreact like he did at times.

"What's up baby," he sounded excited to hear my voice.

"Well, I have some not-so-great news. Sam came up to the salon today."

"What!" He yelled out. "See, he's going to make me hurt him. I'm trying to do the right thing by becoming a Christian. I go to church every Sunday I'm trying to live right and the devil won't stop testing me. Where are you right now?"

"I'm at the bakery picking up the cake for the party."

"Stay there, I'm on my way to come and get you, I'm not cool with you going anywhere by yourself until I've gotten this situation straightened out."

"Trey, you bugging, you ain't going to be able to come everywhere with me."

"Well at least until we get a restraining order on that fool. That's the only way I'm going to feel comfortable."

"I don't think that it's necessary to follow me around everywhere; besides all I have to do is make one more stop to the party store to pick up some decorations. As soon as I'm done I'll be heading home."

"I think you are being hardheaded, which you often are at times, but I'll let you do you, but you know how I feel about the situation."

"I know baby, but I will be fine, trust me. I will be home in time to make you and Adrianna some dinner."

"You got your mace and you still have me on speed dial, right?"

"Yes Trey of course, I'll see you in a little bit."

When I was done purchasing my items I put my bags in the trunk and I immediately checked all four of my tires to make sure they weren't slashed. All four tires were intact but my car door was open. That's strange, I thought to myself as I got in and started up the car. Next thing I knew a hand was covering my mouth. When I turned around it was Sam. He was hiding in the back of my car seat. "Shhhh," he said as he grabbed my arm with his other hand.

"I didn't want to go about things this way but you left me no choice. You might be mad at me for now but you will see this is best for you. We're gonna start all over and have us a family."

"Let me go," I screamed. I was trying to fight with my free arm. Next thing I knew he pulled out a gun.

"I mean business Chrissie, be quiet," he said as he grabbed me by the hair so hard I felt my eyes tighten.

Damn, if only I would have listened to my husband, I thought to myself.

"Move to the passenger side right now," he ordered. I hurried and did what I was told; I could see his patience wearing thin. He hopped in the driver's seat.

I then saw Trey pulling up, it was a good thing he didn't listen to me and he came for me anyway. I started banging on the car windows but he didn't hear me. Then Sam pulled off. As soon as Sam was pulling off, Trey spotted me and he saw that Sam was driving my car. He jumped back in his car to follow us but Sam was too far ahead and there was no way Trey was going to catch up with him; he still tried anyway. Then I saw the worst thing possible happened: I saw Trey get into a head-on collision with another car.

I screamed as loudly as I possibly could. "I hate you Sam, I hate you, what if he's dead?" I cried. "You and I would never be together, don't you see that?" Tears kept rolling down my face as I replayed the accident over and over in my head. "Who's going to take care of Adrianna?" I said as I sobbed.

"Your mom and your sister for now until you come to your senses. Then she can live with us and we'll be a happy family."

I could tell at any moment I was going to have a full-on panic attack. I took in a few deep breaths and exhaled slowly.

"Where are you taking me?"

"We're going to a hotel room until I figure everything out."

"Everything like what?"

"Well now, since I may be facing kidnapping charges, I say we will get some disguises and move out of the state."

"Out of the state?" I screamed. I started to have a panic attack all over again. I couldn't take the fact that I didn't know if my husband was dead or alive.

We finally pulled up to the motel, and Sam put the gun to my head once more. "Don't try any funny shit,"

When we walk to the room he handed me a jacket with a hood. I felt a little better when he put the gun away. I kept looking around the room and I was trying to come up with some ways to escape.

"Are you hungry?" he asked.

"You're asking me am I hungry? I just got kidnapped, I don't know if my husband is dead or alive; no, I'm not fucking hungry."

"Well, do you need anything else?"

"What I need you ain't willing to give me so I don't even know why you're asking."

"I got a blonde wig and some clothes for you to put on," he said as he tried on a few wigs for his disguise.

"I know you don't agree with me but in the end you'll see that this is what's best for you. Now I need you to cooperate. I don't want to do anything to hurt you, I love you."

"You don't want to hurt her but I do," yelled out an angry Ramona as she busted into the room.

I should have been happy to see her so that this whole kidnapping would be over, but she looked pissed and she looked like she had murder in her eyes.

"You lowdown dirty dog, why couldn't you just leave this young bitch alone? I'm going to kill your ass Cristina. I swear you caused my family too much pain. You ruined my marriage and my sister Veronica is locked up for life.

"Veronica's your sister?" I was now really confused.

"Yes, and she said you came to L.A. and tried to steal her man also."

"She is the one who set Chris up and had him killed and she tried to frame me for it and I had to do time in that hellhole."

Sam was looking at us both confused. He still had his gun facing Ramona and Ramona still had her gun facing me and I was caught in the middle of these two mad people. She then turned the gun away from me and she turned it on him.

"And Sam how could you? You got that gun pointed to me, your wife, instead of this bitch. You promised me that you would never do this to me again. You already gave me a mental breakdown. You are a liar. Now you done kidnapped her so that you can do what? Run away with her so that the two of you can be happily ever after? Over my dead body. I'm going do us both a favor, Now say goodbye to your mistress Chrissie,"

Before she could finish, the police opened the doors and shot her in the back.

"No," cried Sam. He ran to Ramona and started crying. "I'm so sorry I didn't mean for this to happen to you. You weren't supposed to follow me down here," he said, sobbing like a girl.

The police instantly slapped the cuffs on Sam. "What're you guys arresting me for? I didn't kill anybody."

"You are under arrest for kidnapping," said the officer as he escorted Sam to the police car. The coroner came shortly after to take Ramona's body away.

"Are you okay?" asked another officer who was present on the scene.

"Yes, I'm fine but my husband was in a bad car crash following behind me. I need to know if he's okay." I sound really desperate.

"Well your husband is the one who informed us about the kidnapping. He knew the man's full name and he gave us a description and the license plate's number. It just so happened an officer was in the area."

"You guys made it just in time. How's my husband doing?"

"Well see, that's the bad news. He may not make it. His injuries are very serious. He had just enough in him to report everything he knew."

"Can someone get me to the hospital as soon as possible? I need to be with him."

When I got to the hospital it brought tears to my eyes to see my husband bandaged up with tubes taped all over him. I couldn't help but to feel like everything was my fault. I should have obeyed him instead of being hardheaded.

A tear rolled down my cheek as I kissed him on the forehead. He suddenly opened his eyes. He was in no position to talk but he grabbed my hand and he squeezed it, letting me know that he felt my presence.

After my visit was over, the doctor wanted to check me out to make sure I was all right. She checked my heartbeat; blood pressure and she did a few other tests.

"Looks like I got some news for you," said the nurse with a smile.

"What's the news?" I asked.

"Looks like you're expecting."

"Are you serious?"

"You're at least seven weeks," she said.

"Trey was just bringing up the fact that he wanted another kid."

After the doctor finished checking me out, I went to sit back with my husband.

"Trey, listen to me. I need you now more than ever; you have to fight because you're going to be a daddy again. I don't want this child to end up like I did when my daddy was killed when I was in my mom's womb. I need you to fight for me baby, please. I love you," I told him as I kissed his forehead.

I believe that night Trey heard me tell him that he was going to be a dad because as the days went on he was making progress. By the fourth day the doctors said he'd made major improvements. That night he spoke for the first time since he'd been in the hospital.

"I love you. Take care of yourself and our baby," was all he said before drifting back off to sleep.

Each passing day he got stronger and stronger. A week later he was out of the hospital. He was going to be on crutches for a while but that didn't matter; I was going to stick by his side even if he would have to be in a wheelchair.

Even though so much happened, we still were going to give Mrs. Jenkins that surprise party. Mom went to pick her up from her home. She lied and told her that we had dinner reservations for her.

"Surprise!" everyone yelled.

She looked confused. "They talking to me?" she asked my mom.

"Yes, they are talking to you."

Everyone went to hug and kiss her. She had plenty of gifts awaiting her.

We sang and dance ate and we watched her open all her gifts. It was a good thing to see all of our family together with Mrs. Jenkins.

I hugged and kissed my husband and I silently thanked God for keeping him alive.

"You're still the most handsome man in the world, even on crutches," I told him.

"You better stop all of that sweet talk. You're gonna get it when you get home; these crutches ain't gonna stop nothing."

"You're so silly," I said as I kissed him on the lips.

"I love you, wife."

"I love you too, husband."

...The End